She was going to die...like Tessa.

She couldn't let that happen.

Brooke's training kicked in. She aimed her fingers at his face and eye-balled him. His grip loosened and she slipped from his grasp, scrambled to the other side of the car and dug her Glock from the glove box. She turned to face him but came up empty. She spotted him running around a corner of the garage.

She lowered her gun and fought to catch her breath.

Realization struck her. She'd come to Tessa's place of employment looking for answers to her cousin's murder. She'd been attacked herself. Could this attack be tied to Tessa's murder? It had to be. As she waited for the police to arrive, she thought about the photograph of Tessa and Colby on the desk. If this attack had something to do with Tessa, Brooke needed Colby Avery's help. She had to get answers about her cousin's death before the killer struck again.

Virginia Vaughan is a born-and-raised Mississippi girl. She is blessed to come from a large Southern family, and her fondest memories include listening to stories recounted around the dinner table. She was a lover of books from a young age, devouring tales of romance, danger and love. She soon started writing them herself. You can connect with Virginia through her website, virginiavaughanonline.com, or through the publisher.

Books by Virginia Vaughan

Love Inspired Suspense

Cowboy Lawmen

Texas Twin Abduction
Texas Holiday Hideout
Texas Target Standoff
Texas Baby Cover-Up
Texas Killer Connection

Covert Operatives

Cold Case Cover-Up
Deadly Christmas Duty
Risky Return
Killer Insight

Visit the Author Profile page at LoveInspired.com.

TEXAS KILLER CONNECTION

VIRGINIA VAUGHAN

LOVE INSPIRED SUSPENSE
INSPIRATIONAL ROMANCE

LOVE INSPIRED® SUSPENSE

INSPIRATIONAL ROMANCE

ISBN-13: 978-1-335-55501-4

Texas Killer Connection

Copyright © 2022 by Virginia Vaughan

For questions and comments about the quality of this book, please contact us at CustomerService@Harlequin.com.

Love Inspired
22 Adelaide St. West, 41st Floor
Toronto, Ontario M5H 4E3, Canada
www.LoveInspired.com

Printed in U.S.A.

But now, O Lord, thou art our father; we are the clay, and thou our potter; and we all are the work of thy hand.
—Isaiah 64:8

This book is lovingly dedicated to my mom, Sylvia. You've been my biggest cheerleader, my confidante and my friend. You've helped me plot, listened to me gripe when a story wouldn't come together and even helped me figure out where to hide the bodies. You help bring my stories to life and I'm thankful. I love you.

ONE

Voice mail again.

Brooke Moore ended the call without leaving a message. She'd already left three for FBI Agent Colby Avery. He had yet to respond. She jammed her cell phone into her purse, removed the keys from the ignition and got out. She'd been back in Dallas for three days and had visited the police to find answers about her cousin's murder. They'd referred her to the FBI, who'd given her Colby Avery's contact information, but he wasn't returning her calls. Now it was time to visit Tessa's workplace.

She exited the parking garage and walked to the main entrance of the hospital where Tessa had worked as an internal medicine doctor until her murder four months earlier. Four months, and there were still no answers about who had killed Tessa or why.

A pang of regret gripped Brooke as she walked through the automatic doors and into the place where Tessa had spent most of her time. Demanding jobs had kept them apart for years, and months had passed without them speaking. Now, Tessa was gone. She would never speak to her cousin again.

Brooke walked to the information desk and asked to speak with Director Winters. She'd phoned earlier to set up the meeting with Tessa's boss. The woman at the desk glanced up, shock and surprise filling her expression. Brooke pushed a strand of her dark hair behind her ear. She'd expected this. She and Tessa had looked alike. A lot. Their mothers had been identical twins, and that had resulted in an uncanny resemblance between Brooke and her cousin. A resemblance that could cause quite a stir at Tessa's place of employment where everyone knew about her death. The woman fumbled with the phone as she placed a call and then directed Brooke to take the main elevators to the second floor.

She strode through the lobby, bracing herself for the expected reaction. People stopped and gawked at her, confusion clouding their faces, but no one spoke or asked who she was. She made it to a suite of offices on the second floor and received the same shocked expression from Director Caroline Winters.

The director's jaw dropped open and her eyes widened when Brooke entered her office.

Brooke held out her hand to introduce herself. "My name is Brooke Moore. I'm Tessa's cousin."

The woman quickly composed herself when Brooke stated her name. "Yes, of course. Please take a seat."

Brooke settled into a chair across from her. "Thank you for seeing me."

"Of course. Dr. Morgan—Tessa—was a much beloved member of the medical team. Everyone here misses her, especially her patients."

"Thank you for saying that." She appreciated the woman's kind words but had no time for small talk. "I've been to the police. They told me the FBI has taken over the case but wouldn't tell me why. Do you know what's going on?"

"I don't. Unfortunately, we've also been left in the dark about the investigation. Until last week, we weren't even allowed to enter her office. They had it cordoned off and wouldn't release it."

"It's still vacant? May I see it?" A chance to see her cousin's office had her heart racing. It might provide the answers she sought.

"Certainly." The director stood, led her out, and motioned to the right. "This way."

They garnered stares from people as they walked. Director Winters shot her an apologetic look. "I'm sorry for the way people are reacting. As I said, people here really loved Tessa. She was friendly with everyone, doctors, nurses, maintenance and service workers. They all loved her. Seeing you…"

Yes, she'd sensed it before. They thought they were seeing a dead woman walking. "It's no problem. I understand."

"I imagine you and Tessa got stares all the time when you were together."

"We did." Her heart ached at the realization that that would never happen again. She and Tessa had always been as close as sisters. They'd gotten used to the attention their resemblance garnered as kids, but as adults, they'd each tried to forge their own individual lives and careers. Tessa as a physician, and Brooke through her work with INSCOM—the U.S. Army Intelligence and Security Command.

"Tessa told me you worked overseas. Will you be going back there or staying in town?"

Texas hadn't been her home for years, not since she'd joined the army at nineteen. But the army wasn't her home any longer, not since her relationship with her boyfriend and supervisor, Jack Miller, failed. His infidelity had stabbed at her, but his keeping Tessa's death from her had been the final blow to her feelings for him. She couldn't trust him enough to be in a relationship, and she certainly couldn't work with him any longer. She'd made the decision not to reenlist when her time was up next month. But Texas held nothing for her either, not with Tessa gone.

"I'm not going anywhere until I figure out what happened to my cousin and bring her killer to justice." Once that was done, she would figure out her next move.

"What about the police and the FBI? Shouldn't you let them handle the investigation?"

"It's been months and they haven't accomplished anything. Besides, I have information they don't." She knew her cousin better than strangers—even ones with law enforcement training. Hopefully, she could piece together Tessa's last days and uncover who had killed her and why.

They rounded a corner and nearly ran into a slender woman with dark hair and glasses. Director Winters grabbed her arm to steady them both. "Sheila, you startled me. I didn't hear you coming."

"I didn't hear you either. I'm sorry." She turned to look at Brooke, and her eyes widened.

Director Winters was quick to try to alleviate her surprise. "Let me introduce you to Brooke Moore. She's Dr. Morgan's cousin. Sheila works next door at Health-max. They handle all of our billing."

Brooke reached to shake her hand. "It's nice to meet you, Sheila."

The woman still seemed a bit shaken by the resemblance, but she took Brooke's hand. "You too."

"I take it you knew my cousin?"

"Yes, I did. She was a nice lady. We'd become good friends over the past few months. In fact, I was just leaving flowers by her office door."

Director Winters turned to Brooke. "The staff has been doing that as sort of a memorial since she died. As I said, everyone liked her."

"When was the last time you saw her?"

"A few days before she was killed. I was supposed to meet with her the night she died—she was helping me fill out some paperwork for grad school—but my boyfriend, Ross, surprised me with a date night, so I had to cancel. I can't help but think she might still be alive if I hadn't."

Brooke understood. She had her own set of regrets when it came to Tessa. "You can't blame yourself. You weren't responsible. The person who killed her is the one who should feel guilty. Don't worry. I'm going to find him and make certain he pays for what he did."

Sheila pushed her glasses up on her nose. "I should get back to work. It was nice to meet you, Brooke."

"You too."

Sheila hurried away, and Brooke and Director Winters continued down the hallway. They approached a door where, as the director had stated, flowers and cards lined the wall. A swell of emotion hit Brooke. It was nice to know her cousin had had people who cared so much about her.

She reached out to touch the nameplate on the door: Tessa Morgan, MD.

I won't give up on you, Tessa. I will find out what happened to you.

Director Winters unlocked the door, pushed it open and switched on the overhead lights. Boxes sat beneath the windows on the outside wall, and the bookshelves had been mostly cleared. "I had maintenance in here boxing up her personal items, but I see they haven't finished. Of course, the FBI seized most of her personal files."

Brooke walked to the desk and sat in the chair. Hot tears threatened to break through, but she choked them back. She'd dreaded coming here for this very reason. Everything around her, from the books to the paintings on the wall, the plants in the window to the photographs on her desk, were all Tessa. A wave of grief so strong it nearly knocked her over swept through her.

"Why don't I give you a minute?" Director Winters offered.

Brooke wanted to thank her but feared she would break down if she did, so she only nodded. She couldn't let her grief overwhelm her, not if she hoped to find answers about Tessa's murder.

A picture on the desk caught her eye. Tessa smiling, her arms around a man with a handsome face and piercing blue eyes. They looked happy.

Pain gripped her. It had been months since she'd spoken to her cousin, so this relationship had to be new. She reached out and outlined Tessa's image. She was happy her cousin had found love in her last days, but it also reminded her of her own pain and heartbreak. Jack's infidelity had ended their two-year relationship. Then, as if he could sink any lower, he'd kept Tessa's death from her for weeks, rationalizing that it would put her undercover mission with INSCOM at risk.

Brooke had been heartbroken and decided then and there not to re-up when her discharge date arrived. She had enough leave saved up to cover her time off from now until her release and had no desire to return to army life or to Jack.

This photograph was a new clue. She needed to find this mysterious boyfriend in the picture. He could know more about Tessa's death and might be able to provide some answers. Brooke read the notation written in Tessa's hand in the corner: *Me and Colby. Beach trip. Summer.*

Colby Avery? That could explain the FBI's involvement. Had her cousin been dating an FBI agent?

She jumped to her feet, grabbed her purse and stuffed the photo into it. If Colby Avery wouldn't respond to her calls, she would track the man down.

She rushed from the hospital, pulling out her phone

and dialing the number her contact at the FBI had given her for Colby. Once again, the call went straight to voice mail. Frustrated, she left another message. "Agent Avery, this is Brooke Moore again. I need to speak with you about my cousin Tessa's murder. Please call me."

Why wasn't he returning her calls? There had to be another way to reach him. She could call one of her friends in the intelligence community who could probably uncover his address. It wasn't a step she would normally take, but for Tessa, she would do whatever it took to contact him.

Her steps faltered as a chill crept up her spine. The army had honed her instincts, and she wasn't about to ignore her internal voice. Her hand itched for her gun, but she'd stowed it in her car earlier before her trip to the FBI offices and left it there due to hospital rules.

Unable to shake the feeling she was being watched, she quickened her pace. She clicked the key fob on her rental car and opened the door. The image of a man standing behind her reflected in the window. He grabbed her before she could react, pressing his hand over her nose and mouth.

Her assailant squeezed so hard that her breath caught. Her vision blurred and the ground tilted. She had to break free of this guy's hold before she lost consciousness. The man's hot breath singed her neck.

She was going to die…like Tessa.

She couldn't let that happen.

Her training kicked in. She pressed her feet against the car and braced herself. She aimed her fingers at his face and eye-balled him. His grip loosened and she slipped from his grasp, scrambled to the other side of the car and dug her Glock from the glove box. She turned to face him but came up empty. She spotted him running around a corner of the garage.

She lowered her gun and fought to catch her breath. Hands shaking, she leaned against the car and struggled to call the police.

Realization struck her. She'd come to Tessa's place of employment looking for answers to her cousin's murder. She'd been attacked herself. Could this attack be tied to Tessa's murder? It had to be. But why now? Four months after Tessa's death? Had the assailant mistaken Brooke for her cousin? She shook her head, dismissing that idea. Tessa was dead. No one would know that better than the person who had murdered her. But as she waited for the police to arrive, she thought about the photograph of Tessa and Colby on the desk. If this attack had something to do with Tessa, Brooke needed Colby Avery's help. She had to get answers about her cousin's death before the killer struck again.

He was late.

Colby rubbed his still-stubbly face as he climbed into his pickup and headed into town to meet his brother, Josh, for breakfast. It was getting harder and harder to pull himself awake in the mornings after spending hours at night staring at his evidence board and trying to force himself to see some connection that would break Tessa's murder case. His family called him obsessed, but how could he not be?

Four months. That's how long a killer had gone free

without repercussions. So far, there wasn't a thing he could do about it. He knew the culprit or, at least, the man who'd hired the killer. He'd known from the day some unsuspecting soul had discovered Tessa's body on the side of a road that John Dutton, CEO and founder of Healthmax Financial Company, was responsible.

Dutton's company handled the healthcare billing services for private providers as well as the hospital where Tessa had worked as a doctor. Tessa had called Colby, claiming she had documentation that Healthmax had been using her name and medical provider number to file fraudulent claims. Colby had been out of town when she'd called, so he'd encouraged her to gather more evidence before he contacted the FBI's White-Collar Crime Unit once he returned to town. That had been a mistake.

Tessa had left him a message saying she suspected someone from the company was on to her. She'd made a copy of her documentation and hidden it in case something happened to her. And it had. She had been found murdered days later, and her documentation was missing. They'd found nothing at the crime scene that could tie Dutton to the murder. The man had killed a witness and gotten away with it.

Colby gripped the steering wheel. *Not for long. Enjoy your freedom, Dutton, because I'm coming for you.*

He rounded the curve that took him to the town square and veered right toward Faye's Diner. An image in his rearview mirror grabbed his attention. His heart raced. He slammed on the brakes and spun around in his seat to scan the sidewalk behind him. He steadied his breathing as he saw... Well, nothing out of the ordinary.

For a fleeting moment, he would have sworn he'd seen Tessa. He scanned the street again and then righted in his seat and tried to push the image from his mind as his heartbeat slowly returned to normal. He had to have imagined it. Tessa was dead.

A horn honked and he saw a car had pulled up behind him. He'd stopped in the middle of the road. In Dallas, he would have been crashed into by traffic, but not in his hometown of Courtland, Texas. He pulled the car to the curb and parked. Walking the few remaining blocks to Faye's would give him the opportunity to clear his head.

He spotted Cecile Richardson, Josh's chief investigator, through the window of the diner. As sheriff of Courtland County, Josh relied on Cecile, and they were the closest of friends, but today, Cecile's face was hard and set. She pointed a finger at Josh and spoke words Colby couldn't make out before sliding from the booth and walking off. Colby opened the door for her and she whizzed right past him without a word. He'd known Cecile for years, and she always had a friendly smile. Not today. Whatever had happened had her rattled.

Colby walked into the diner, slipped into her spot in the booth and studied his brother, who leaned on his elbows and looked defeated. "What was that about?"

Josh took a deep breath and then pulled himself together "Nothing. Just some stuff between us. We'll work it out."

Colby waved to the waitress and asked for coffee. Josh's guarded expression told him something was up with him and Cecile. He didn't know if it had something to do with work at the sheriff's office or something personal. Given his brother's guarded response, he didn't want to pry. He knew from experience the kind of icy distance he'd seen between them often stemmed from personal issues not professional ones.

Josh pushed a hand through his hair and gave a loud sigh before turning his attention to Colby. "How are you doing?"

Colby had returned home two months ago when his investigation into Tessa's death had stalled and his boss, Greg Sanders, had insisted he was too close to it. Greg had suggested Colby take time off to clear his head and grieve, so he'd come back to his family's Texas ranch to lick his wounds. But he couldn't rest knowing that Dutton had gotten away with murder.

"Have you given any thought to going back to work?"

Colby shook his head. "I'm not ready, not after what happened with Kellyanne."

Josh leaned forward. "That wasn't your fault, Colby."

"I led her attackers to her." As if he'd needed any more proof that his judgment had been compromised, less than a day after returning to Courtland, he'd led armed men to the fishing cabin where his sister, the man who was now her husband, and the baby they'd adopted had been hiding out after being hunted by a killer trying to make the infant disappear to cover up an affair with his murdered mother. The child had been abducted, and although they were able to retrieve him and their sister, Kellyanne, safely, Colby still kicked himself for allowing it. He hadn't seen the tail. He'd been trained better than that, but he'd allowed his grief over Tessa to cloud his conviction. He'd thought he was getting better. Until today. Until minutes ago.

Might as well admit what had happened. "That's not all. On the way over here, I thought I saw Tessa." He pulled his cup to his lips and then paused as he spotted a figure walking down the sidewalk outside the diner. Her wavy dark hair was familiar, as was her athletic body and sharp, beautiful features.

He closed his eyes then opened them again. They had to be playing tricks on him. But she was still there, crossing the street and heading toward a parked car.

The same woman he'd seen earlier in his rearview mirror.

"Tessa!" He dropped his cup and leaped from the seat, running to the exit. Josh rushed out behind him as Colby crossed the street, calling her name. "Tessa!"

She stopped walking and his pulse sped up. Even with her back to him, he knew it was her. But how?

She turned to face him and time stood still.

"Colby." She said his name as her lips turned upward into a half smile, but his name sounded wrong coming from her mouth.

A van skidded to a stop in front of her, and a man jumped out and tackled her, shoving her into the open vehicle.

Colby pulled his gun and ran after them, yelling, "FBI!"

Her scream echoed in his ears.

He'd lost her again.

The weight of her assailant slammed into Brooke. She hit the floor of the van with a sickening thud.

He shouted to the driver, "Go, go, go!"

The vehicle roared forward, sending Brooke rolling from the force.

Someone shouted at them, and then gunfire sounded. Her assailant swore and hollered for the driver to go faster.

Brooke didn't know who was doing the shooting, and she didn't care. After the initial shock of being ambushed, her senses returned in full force. Pain radiated up through her leg from it being rammed against the van as her attacker shoved her inside. Her instincts kicked in as her danger alert sounded. These people were more than likely the ones who'd killed Tessa. She had to get away before they did the same to her.

The man tried to yank the door closed but Brooke's legs blocked him. He tried to pull them in, and she kicked him. He tumbled backward from the force. She flung herself through the open door to freedom.

Her head hit the hard asphalt. Starbursts lit her vision as pain pulsed through her so intense she couldn't even decipher which area of her body hurt more. She looked up. The van screeched to a stop and the man stumbled out. He was coming after her. She had to get out of there.

Sirens wailed, causing her abductor to hop back into the van. It took off, tires squealing. Relief swept through her as the sirens closed in. Two police cruisers sped past her in pursuit, but a third stopped.

A man jumped out and ran to her. "Are you okay?"

She almost couldn't hear the question over the ringing in her ears but she saw him mouth the words as she stared into his strong face, intense blue eyes and worried expression. He seemed familiar, but from where? Oh yes, Colby. Colby Avery, the FBI agent. The man in Tessa's picture. She'd come here to find him. Tessa's boyfriend. She'd tracked him down to find answers about her cousin's death.

Brooke tried to assure him she was okay. She was beaten up and in pain but glad to be free from her attackers.

Colby took her hand. She only heard about every third word he said as the ringing in her ears died down, but she heard the name Tessa.

No, no, no.

He thought she was Tessa. No wonder his face had registered shock when she'd turned to him.

He touched her face and brushed a handful of hair out of her eyes. A rush of electricity ran through her as his finger stroked her skin.

Whoa. Slow down, Brooke. This is Tessa's boyfriend. She pushed his hand away. "This is a mistake." She struggled to sit but the world spun at her attempt and nausea rolled through her. She fell back to the asphalt.

All the sounds around her mushed together into one loud ringing noise. Whoever had attacked her in the parking garage must have followed her here to Courtland. He'd been watching her and she hadn't noticed. She'd been on high alert after the attack in the parking garage, so how had this man followed her all the way to Courtland without her catching a glimpse of him?

Confusion and worry clouded Colby's face. She wanted to assure him she wasn't who he thought she was, but everything around her was fading fast. The only thing she was super aware of was her hand in his as darkness pulled her under.

Colby paced the waiting room floor.

His mind spun with confusion. How could Tessa be lying in a bed here in Courtland? It didn't make any sense.

Josh sat in one of the chairs lining the wall of the waiting room. "Could it have been witness protection?" His brother was throwing out ideas, like Colby, trying to make sense of this. There had to be an explanation.

"I saw her body, Josh. She was dead. I don't understand how she can be here."

The doors opened and a nurse stepped into the waiting area and motioned to him. "She's awake."

He gulped back a lump that had formed in his throat at the thought of not being able to get the answers he desired. "Can I see her?"

Josh stood, making certain his badge was showing. "I need to take her statement about the attempted abduction. Can she do that?"

"Yes, she seems very coherent and alert. We want to keep her overnight for observation since she lost consciousness, but she's resisting."

Colby nearly said he would talk her into staying but bit his tongue before he did. It wasn't his place to tell her to stay, though he was going to do everything in his power to convince her to do just that. He wouldn't let anything else happen to her on his watch.

The nurse pointed the way to the door, and Colby

and Josh entered the room. The familiar figure lay on the bed, bandages on her arms and neck. Her dark hair hung loose and wavy, gutting his heart in its familiarity, but the moment she looked at him, something was different. Her eyes were green instead of brown, and the way she held the paper cup of water in her hand was different. If she was an imposter, her disguise was nearly perfect, but not perfect enough.

This woman wasn't Tessa.

"Who are you?" he asked, his breath catching as he spoke the words.

She set down the cup of water and her green eyes watched him. "My name is Brooke Moore."

He felt his shoulders sag at the confirmation that she was not Tessa. He'd known it in his heart, but that last piece of hope shattered. Tessa was dead. How did this woman look so much like her?

He pulled a hand through his hair as he stared at her. How was it possible? Tessa had been an only child. She'd told him she didn't have any family except a cousin in the military. His mind went back to those conversations. They'd grown up like sisters. Brooke. Her cousin Brooke.

"You're Tessa's cousin?"

"Yes. She told you about me?"

She had but… "She never told me you looked so much alike."

She gave a small smile. "Our mothers were identical twins. We've always favored each other."

"It's more than that, Brooke. You and Tessa could be twins yourself."

"I know. I'm sorry to spring this on you."

"I wasn't expecting it. That's all. I thought I was seeing Tessa, but I knew that couldn't be true. I saw her body. I buried her. But…seeing you… I thought—"

"I know what you thought." She fingered her cup and looked up at him again. "I've been out of the country. It took me a while to get back to the States after I learned my cousin was dead. Murdered. I went to the FBI to try to find out what happened to her, but they wouldn't tell me anything. They claim it's an open investigation and they can't share the details, but Greg Sanders suggested I contact you."

He was surprised Greg would suggest that, but he was glad. Technically, he was still the lead on Tessa's case, and he could understand her cousin wanting to know what had happened to her.

He just wished he had those answers to give.

"I tried calling you. I left multiple voice mail messages, but you never responded." Her tone held a bite to it that filled him with shame. His phone had been stuck in a drawer for weeks. It hadn't occurred to him that anyone besides family would need to get in touch.

"Maybe you two could talk more about that tomorrow when Brooke is released," Josh suggested.

Colby had forgotten he was even here in the room.

He continued, moving toward the bed and pulling out his notebook. "For now, we need to focus on what happened today. I'm Sheriff Josh Avery. Do you feel up to giving me a statement?"

She nodded and took another sip from her cup as Josh took a seat in the chair beside the hospital bed.

"Did you recognize the men who tried to abduct you?"

"No. The one who grabbed me wore a mask. I didn't get a good look at the driver, but I heard her voice. It sounded like a woman's."

Josh looked at Colby. He knew they were thinking the same thing. A team. These people had come at Brooke as a team.

"I arrived in town about an hour earlier. I had an address for Silver Star Ranch, but my GPS took me in circles, so I stopped at a café on the corner to ask if anyone knew Colby."

"That must have been when I saw you," Colby stated. "I thought I was losing my mind. I knew you couldn't be Tessa. When I looked again, you were gone."

Josh steered the conversation back to the matter at hand. "Any idea what they wanted from you?"

"Today wasn't the first time someone has targeted me. I was attacked when I visited my cousin's office yesterday. I was able to fight my way free."

Like she'd done today. Impressive.

"The police took a report and gathered fingerprints, but they weren't able to identify the man who tried to grab me. I suspected it had something to do with Tessa's murder, but now that he's followed me here to Courtland, I'm certain of it. I think whoever killed Tessa now wants me dead too."

Josh scowled at her hasty determination. "Wait a minute. Let's not jump to conclusions. You said you've been out of the country. Doing what? Could there be someone in your past who might want to harm you?

Could these attacks have to do with something in your personal or professional life?"

She shook her head. "I don't know of anyone who would want to hurt me. I worked in army intelligence. Most of what I did was classified. As for a personal life, my last relationship is still stationed overseas. He can't be involved. This must have something to do with Tessa. I only just arrived in Texas a few days ago."

"I still need to rule out those possibilities." Josh closed his notebook and stood. He didn't look convinced. "I'll head back to the office and see if there have been any sightings on that van. I put out a BOLO for it. I've also requested any surveillance videos from the surrounding businesses and have my deputies canvassing the crowd to see if anyone saw someone suspicious hanging around. I'll let you both know if we find any useful information. Maybe we can capture these guys before they flee town."

Dread filled Colby. If what she said was true and these attacks had nothing to do with her, Brooke had somehow stumbled into the path of Tessa's killer either because of the resemblance or by her actions. It was the only thing that made sense.

He couldn't allow what happened to Tessa happen to Brooke. Protecting Brooke wouldn't bring Tessa back, but it was the least he could do for her memory.

TWO

Brooke's head still pounded and the memory of being shoved into that van kept replaying in her mind. The shock, the fear… Was that how her cousin had felt in her last moments? She shuddered, grateful Colby and his brother had left and weren't here to see it.

She couldn't allow herself to get emotional. She had a job to do. She needed to figure out who had killed her cousin and bring him to justice.

She had another issue too. Her reaction to Colby Avery was something she hadn't expected. Her face still felt warm from where Colby had touched it hours earlier and, when he'd walked into her hospital room, she'd been struck by his intense blue eyes and strong, square features. No wonder Tessa had fallen for the handsome agent. But she'd come here looking for justice, not romance. She had to keep her focus.

She stared at the phone on the bedside table. Despite what she'd told the brothers, she should call Jack to let him know what was happening in case this did lead back to her work in the army. *Stop it.* She scolded herself for even thinking about picking up the phone. These attacks had nothing to do with Jack and her work overseas. The absence of him in her life stung. Jack had been her best friend for years, so when their friendship had blossomed into something more, she'd been happy. But he'd betrayed her in the worst way with his unfaithfulness and by keeping Tessa's death from her. He'd received the notification weeks before but had failed to pass it on to her or pull her out of an undercover assignment.

She'd missed Tessa's funeral. Even if she could find a way to forgive Jack's infidelity, how could she ever forgive him for that?

Tears pressed against her eyes. She slid beneath the covers and let them come. She would need to keep her emotions in check if she was going to work with Colby to find her cousin's killer. That meant only getting as close to Colby Avery as necessary to solve the case.

I'm sorry I missed your funeral, Tessa. I'm sorry I wasn't there for you.

A wave of loneliness washed over her. She'd left behind her career and her boyfriend, and now Tessa was gone too.

All she had left was justice.

Nothing could get in the way of that.

Colby sat on the bed in the spare bedroom at his brother's cabin and stared at the evidence board he'd created. It held all the information he'd collected in the course of his investigation into Tessa's murder. There were so many strings that went nowhere. So many unanswered questions and dead ends. He'd prayed for God to give him some guidance in solving it. He hadn't expected the answer to his prayer to come from a walking, talking lookalike of his dead former girlfriend, but the unexpected arrival of Tessa's cousin could finally move the case forward after months of being at a standstill.

He didn't know what answers Brooke could provide, but she'd already done more to lure the killer out just by her presence than he'd been able to accomplish in the past four months. That, in itself, was enough for him to commit to working with her.

He stepped into the hallway when he heard the front door open and close, and headed toward the living room. "What did you find?"

Josh tossed his cowboy hat onto the kitchen counter. "You know, if I hadn't had to pull information on Brooke Moore for the incident today, I wouldn't have even checked into her background. As it is, you shouldn't be granted access to it."

"Then why are you letting me?"

"Because I know you, Colby. You won't stop until I do. Plus, I think it's important that you know there's nothing seedy there." He handed Colby the file he held. "It's like she told us. She's worked for army intelligence for twelve years. She's been stationed overseas and got back to the States three days ago. No criminal charges. No suspicious activity in her financials. She seems squeaky clean to me."

Colby let out a sigh of relief. He didn't want to think bad things about Brooke, but his judgment had been off lately. It was good to double-check. He was going to have to depend on this woman to help him get answers. He didn't need any ambiguous issues between them. There was a big enough one there—her exact resemblance to Tessa.

How was he ever going to get past that?

His failure to protect Tessa reflected back at him in Brooke's face. It was all he saw when he looked at her. Tessa might have broken up with him, unable to stomach his dangerous job, but he'd still cared for her. He should have been there for her when she'd needed him.

Josh poured himself a glass of sweet tea from the refrigerator. "Are you going to be able to work with her?"

"This is the first good lead I've had on this case in months. I have no choice but to work with her. I'm glad to know she's on the up-and-up though. Thank you for that."

"You're welcome. I have to admit it's good to see the excitement in your face again."

He was excited. Finally, this case was hot again. "If this guy is in town, if he followed Brooke to Courtland, then he's close. Closer than I've been to him in months. And he's got someone helping him. Brooke can help crack this case."

"How? By being a target?" He set his glass on the counter. "You can't use Brooke to lure the killer out. She needs protecting. She's not bait."

His brother was right. His excitement over finally having a lead in the case had colored his thinking. Brooke needed protection. Whoever was after her had already gotten to Tessa. He couldn't let him hurt Brooke too.

"I've got some work to do at the office. I'll sleep there." Josh picked up his hat and headed for the door.

Josh didn't sleep at the cabin much. His brother practically lived at the sheriff's office, and Colby couldn't blame him. They had something in common. They'd both lost someone to a killer who hadn't been caught. Josh's wife had been murdered right here in this cabin eight years ago. He'd thrown himself into his work but had never been able to bring her murderer to justice. They'd always had a solid relationship as brothers, but Tessa's death had probably cemented their closeness in a way none of his other siblings could understand.

Colby went back to the bedroom and fell onto the bed. He was exhausted from the day's events but excited too. Eventually, sleep would come, but he hadn't had a good night's rest since the murder. He took a deep breath and closed his eyes. He couldn't allow the shroud of fogginess that had taken over his brain affect his ability to keep Brooke safe.

He fell asleep with the same promise he'd made every night since Tessa had died in his head.

I'll find the killer and bring him to justice.

Kyle Redmon, one of Josh's deputies, greeted Colby when he stepped off the elevator at the hospital the next morning. He was glad Josh had thought to immediately post someone at Brooke's door. It hadn't occurred to him. More evidence that he wasn't thinking at his best.

He nodded to Kyle as he approached. "Any problems?"

"Nope, everything's been quiet."

He knocked and then pushed open the door, glad to

see Brooke was up and dressed. Her dark hair flowed across her shoulders as she glanced up at him. His heart skipped a beat. It was eerie how much she reminded him of Tessa.

"How do you feel this morning?"

She shrugged and then slipped on her jacket. "A little achy but nothing that a couple of Tylenol can't fix."

A nurse entered the room and breezed past him. "I've got your discharge papers all ready, hon. I know you're itching to get out of here. Is this handsome fella your ride?" She turned and eyed Colby.

Brooke started to speak but Colby interrupted her in case she was going to suggest calling a cab or something. "Yes, I've got my SUV downstairs and ready to go."

Brooke eyed him for a moment, and he thought she might refuse. She gave a nod of agreement. "Thank you. That'll save us some time."

He went to get his SUV, pulling into the roundabout when the nurse wheeled Brooke out in a wheelchair to meet him. He suspected from the look on her face that she hated being treated like an invalid but had allowed it only because it was hospital policy. Colby jumped out to help her into the front seat of his SUV. No matter what she said, he could see she was still feeling the effects of yesterday's attack. She was limping slightly, and the cuts and scrapes on her face and arms were obvious reminders of the near abduction.

He slid behind the wheel. "Where to?"

"I'd love some food. The hospital breakfast was... Well, hospital food. Plus, I need real coffee."

He drove to Faye's and held her elbow to steady her as they walked inside. All in all, she was strong. He could see that just from their brief encounters.

She slid into one side of a booth and he took the other. April, one of the waitresses he recognized, took their orders and brought them coffee.

Brooke sipped it and gave a loud sigh of satisfaction. "That's more like it. Now, for the reason I came to town. I'd like to know more about how my cousin died."

His heart tightened at that topic. He wanted answers too, but Josh was right. He couldn't let Brooke use herself as bait even if it meant finally finding Tessa's killer. "You've just been through something traumatic, Brooke. It's okay if you want to take some time to recover."

She leaned across the table. "Let's get this one thing straight right now. I did not come here to get to know you better. I want information. I want to find the person who killed my cousin. You're my best chance to make that happen. I don't need coddling, and I don't need you to protect me. I can handle myself."

Fire lit her eyes, and he couldn't stop the smile that curved his lips. He could be overprotective. It was a hazard of the job. Tessa had even called him out on it before. "You sounded just like her right then."

She leaned back in her seat and some of that fire evaporated. "I can hear her saying that too. Neither of us were raised to be very meek."

That much was obvious. "Tessa was the strongest person I knew."

She nodded and blinked back moisture that threatened her eyelashes. "Neither of us ever knew our fathers. When my mom died, I moved in with Tessa and my aunt Kaye. She worked long hours, and we were left alone together a lot to fend for ourselves. It made us both strong and independent."

His family had his back whenever he needed them, but he'd learned over the years that it was a gift not everyone possessed. He'd hated that Tessa'd had no family except for a cousin she hardly ever saw. Now, Brooke didn't even have that. "I cared for her very much." Her death had been like a sucker punch to his soul.

"I saw the photograph of you two at her office. I could tell the feeling was mutual. Tessa looked incredibly happy."

He knew just the photo she was referring to. A day they'd spent at the beach. That had been a good day. He'd been shot in the shoulder a few weeks later while searching for a suspected terrorist in a warehouse raid. Tessa had patched him up, and later, once he'd recovered, she'd ended things between them, claiming his job was just too dangerous for her liking. She hadn't wanted to live her life constantly wondering if he would come home each night.

The irony that she'd been the one killed wasn't lost on him.

Brooke locked eyes with him across the table. "What happened to my cousin?"

Her directness was refreshing. She was a woman who knew what she wanted. Of course, he wasn't supposed to tell her anything. She was the next of kin, and the FBI had protocols, but he owed her the truth. Plus, Greg had sent her his way. That had to count for something. Besides, he wasn't sure that she would let it go if he tried to send her away. And he needed her to know the truth. He needed her help to solve this case.

"Tessa called me a week before she was killed. Said one of her patients had approached her, noticing some unusual charges billed to her insurance. Tessa did some research and found unusual billing practices by the company that handles the hospital's accounts. She believed they were using her name and medical provider number to create fraudulent charges. She said if they were doing it to her, they were surely doing it to other physicians. Our FBI White-Collar Crime Unit takes complaints like that seriously, but I was out of town working another case. I told her to see if she could gather more documentation to back up her claim before I contacted the fraud unit. She agreed to try."

He felt his face warm with shame at the memory. He shouldn't have put her off that way. "She called me again a few days later and left a message. Said she thought someone was on to her and she was scared. She was going to make copies of her documentation and hide it. When I got her messages, I called her back, but she didn't pick up. It was only after I got back into town that I learned the police had found her body."

"You believe whoever was creating those fraudulent accounts killed her?"

"I haven't been able to prove it, but yes. I'm certain the two are connected. Whatever she uncovered, it was enough to get her killed. A lower-level worker wouldn't have a reason to want her dead. But if someone noticed she was snooping around…"

"Her actions probably filtered up to the highest, most corrupt level. Like the CEO?"

He nodded. It was the only working theory he had. "My friend in White-Collar Crime told me that companies like this could rake in millions of dollars by billing for fraudulent charges using multiple provider numbers, and Healthmax had access to hundreds of those numbers through their work with the hospital."

Tears wet her eyes but she pushed them back. He wanted to tell her she needn't bother. He'd seen tears before, and he understood them, but she didn't strike him as the type of person to cry in front of others. She had a strong exterior that reminded him so much of Tessa. But Tessa had been friendly and outgoing. She'd always had a smile for anyone she met. Brooke struck him as quieter and more serious than her cousin. The differences between them fascinated him.

"So you're army intelligence? Is that why you couldn't get back to the States for her funeral?"

She nodded and then sighed. "My commander intercepted the message about Tessa's death. I was undercover at the time, and he didn't want me to know. He thought it would compromise my mission, so he kept it from me."

He cringed at the idea that someone had kept that news from her. Someone she'd trusted. The pain in her voice was evident.

"When I discovered what he'd done, I was so angry. I knew I could never trust him again. I decided right then and there to resign my commission, but I still had some things to work out before I could come home.

There's still paperwork, and I'm technically on leave, but I can't imagine going back." She fingered her coffee cup. "I should have been there for her. We were the only family either one of us had left."

This time, a tear did slip out, but she quickly pushed it away. "So what evidence do you have in my cousin's case?"

"Not much. The last known sighting of her was the night before her body was found. She went to the Emergency Room for a cut on her hand. They stitched it up and she left. That was about nine thirty. They found her body the next morning. The crime scene didn't provide much forensic evidence. Based on that, I don't believe she was killed where she was found. And our auditors haven't found anything unusual at Healthmax. If there was fraud going on, they've covered their tracks."

"What about the documentation Tessa collected? Are you telling me it was worthless?"

"I don't know. We never found it. We searched her office and her apartment. We even went through her computer. Whatever evidence she uncovered, the killer must have taken it with him."

"What about her cell phone? Could it have been stored there?"

"We never found her phone. I set up an alert so that if it becomes active again, we'll know, but so far, nothing. It's still missing. On top of everything else, John Dutton, the CEO of Healthmax had a rock-solid alibi for the night Tessa went missing."

"So then he hired someone to kill her?" The certainty in her voice matched his own.

"We have a lot of theories, but little proof." He leaned back and gave her the truth. "The case has gone cold. The company closed ranks. Dutton even managed to stonewall a second audit with accusations of harassment. The agency backed down."

"So this company is still in business?"

He shared her outrage over that. "Yep. Still defrauding our healthcare system to the tune of hundreds of thousands of dollars."

Fire blazed in her eyes. "They remain in business while my cousin is dead." She shook her head as a new determination settled on her face. "We can't let them get away with that, Colby."

He reached across the table and gave her hand a reassuring squeeze. The softness of her skin both surprised and pleased him. "We won't." And he meant it.

God had sent Brooke to him, and together they would figure this out and find justice for Tessa.

Brooke rubbed her neck and shoulder. The breakfast had been filling, but she was anxious to get started. After what Colby had told her about Tessa's murder, she was ready to learn everything she could about this John Dutton and Healthmax. Only, Colby seemed to be nursing his coffee, taking his sweet time. What was he waiting on?

She couldn't believe she'd told him about Jack. Her only excuse was that she didn't have another good reason for not attending Tessa's funeral. She didn't want Colby to think badly of her. It shouldn't matter what he thought, but something about him made her want to trust him. Tessa had trusted him. But after Jack's betrayal, trust wasn't something that came easily for Brooke.

He set down his cup and sighed. "Why don't we head over to the sheriff's office and see if there's any update on that van or its occupants. It's not far. Just across the square. Are you up for the walk or should I go get the car?"

"I can walk." Her muscles needed a good stretching. Besides, it wouldn't do to appear weak in front of him.

He'd been right when he'd said it wasn't far. Her body protested, but she made the short distance without much difficulty. Thankfully, Colby was beside her if she faltered. She didn't, but it felt good to know he was there just in case.

The town was beautiful. The square boasted a large, historic courthouse in the center with shops surrounding it. A picturesque image of small-town life.

"The sheriff's office is on the side of the courthouse," Colby said.

She spotted his brother the moment they entered the building. Josh stood speaking with a deputy. When they caught his eye, he excused himself and approached her and Colby, his face grim. Not a good sign.

"Any news?" Colby asked.

"Nothing. The van disappeared before my deputies could reach it. We've put out a BOLO to other counties, but so far, no one has reported seeing it. No one we've questioned remembers anything. We're still pulling video surveillance, but the spot where the attack happened was just outside the angle of the bank's camera, and only the opposite side of the van was visible from the hardware store's camera. We weren't able to get an image of the driver or the man who ambushed Brooke."

That wasn't the news she'd hoped to hear. "Surely you have more than two surveillance cameras."

Colby stuffed his hands into his pockets and gave a heavy sigh. "This is a small town, Brooke. A lot of cameras were damaged during the last big storm and haven't been replaced."

"So he gets away with it again?" She didn't like the bitter taste in her mouth. This guy had murdered her cousin and attacked her twice now. They couldn't let him get away with it a third time. "What do we do now?"

"We go back to the drawing board. We start at the beginning with fresh eyes and look at the evidence we have from Tessa's murder."

She realized what Colby was saying. "You're going to let me see the FBI files?"

He gave a slow and cautious nod. This went against everything he believed in. Yet he also wanted justice for Tessa. "It's against FBI policy, and they're not official files, just my copies of them, but I can't discount the possibility that you might be just what we need to crack this case." He looked at his brother. "And I don't mean just as bait."

She didn't understand that jab, but she could guess its meaning and Josh's concern. She didn't care. She would gladly be bait if it meant finding justice for Tessa. The Averys didn't know she could handle herself just fine. She didn't need their kid gloves. Only, now wasn't the time to mention it. Not if she wanted a peek at the evidence Colby had collected in his investigation. "Great, let's get to work. Where are they?"

"At my brother's cabin. I've been staying there since I've been home."

She didn't even feel the aches and pains from her injuries when they climbed into his SUV a few minutes later and headed out of town. She watched the landscape roll by them as he drove. Inside the vehicle, a new excitement was bubbling up between them. She was certain he felt it too. A renewed hope that this case could be solved and Tessa's killer could be brought to justice.

"Thank you for doing this," she told Colby.

"I'm not doing it just for you. I want answers too, Brooke. I need them. This case has turned me inside out. I know every detail back and forth, only none of it makes any sense."

"Maybe you just need a fresh pair of eyes."

He nodded and gave her a smile. "That's what I'm hoping for."

He turned off the main road and parked at an isolated cabin. She didn't see another neighbor anywhere close by but could make out the outline of a barn in the distance. The landscape seemed to go on forever, and the grass and trees were green and lush with everything in bloom. A pleasant flowery fragrance greeted her as she got out of the vehicle.

"It's beautiful here. And so peaceful. This place belongs to your brother?"

"It does. He and his wife built it years ago, but it's still on my family's property. This is all part of our ranch. Silver Star Ranch. There's a path over there lead-ing to the main house, but there is plenty of privacy out here."

"Is his wife home? She doesn't mind you staying with them?"

His eyes clouded over at the question. "Josh is a wid-ower."

"I'm sorry to hear that."

She followed Colby into the cabin where he told her to wait while he went into the back bedroom. He brought out a whiteboard with evidence tacked onto it and leaned it against the couch.

"I thought you might want to see this too."

She glanced at the board and saw it was all related to Tessa's case. "You have been busy."

There was another item in his hand, and he held it out to her. It was a brown file folder with the initials FBI stamped on the front of it. The case file.

She sucked in a breath as she took it from him. Ex-citement flowed through her. Finally, answers.

"I have to warn you that some of this is pretty graphic." Colby rubbed the back of his neck again, and his color changed. He'd been deeply affected by the im-ages and details inside this file.

She hadn't even considered how she would feel reading it. It was going to brutal, but it was necessary. "Thank you."

He placed the evidence board onto the counter, and she snapped a photo of it. She couldn't wait to get some-where and study this file. "I should read this, and then we should meet to talk about it and brainstorm ideas."

He nodded. "That's a good plan. You're not going back to Dallas tonight, are you?"

She glanced at her phone. It was already late, and she was anxious to start reading about Tessa's case. Remaining in town made more sense, especially since she had nothing waiting for her back in Dallas. "I'll get a hotel and stay in town. Can you drive me back to my car?"

"You're welcome to stay here. You can have the bedroom, and I'll take the couch. Josh won't be home. He usually sleeps in town."

"Does he?"

"He hasn't stayed here much since his wife was killed eight years ago. She was murdered in this cabin."

"Did he find the killer?"

"No, but he hasn't given up." He locked eyes with her and his face set into a firm stare. "I won't give up either until I find out who killed Tessa and bring them to justice."

His assurance gave her comfort. She wasn't giving up on this either, and it was good to have another person, an FBI trained investigator, on her side. Only what did it say about his investigative skills that he hadn't been able to crack this case yet? She shook away those doubts. He was obviously just too close to it to be objective. She probably was too, but like Colby, she wouldn't let that stop her from trying.

She also couldn't remain here alone with Colby. His easy smile was making her heart skip a beat and, for all she knew, he'd killed Tessa. Wasn't the boyfriend usually the prime suspect when a woman was murdered?

Stop it. She chided herself for that thought. Colby hadn't attacked her in the hospital parking garage or tried to shove her into a van and abduct her. That was just her mistrust of men that her experience with Jack had instilled in her.

Still, silly or not, she needed some distance from the handsome agent. "I appreciate the offer, but I would feel better staying at a hotel."

His jaw set, but he seemed to understand. "I'll drive you into town."

They climbed into his SUV and headed back the way they'd come. It was a long way to travel to pick up a file, but she was glad they'd made the drive. She couldn't wait to be alone and dive into it.

Colby stopped long enough for her to retrieve her car and then she followed him to a hotel called the Courtland Arms, a five-story building overlooking the town square. She checked in and then turned to say goodbye to Colby.

"I'll walk you to your room," he said before she could.

She wanted to remind him she didn't need his protection, but she liked having him make certain she was safe. It felt good to have someone watching her back again the way Jack had once done. But she'd learned from him that if you allow someone to watch your back, they can easily stab you in it.

Thanks again for that, Jack.

They rode the elevator to the third floor, and Colby followed her to the room at the end of the hall. She unlocked the door and turned to say good-night.

"I'll look over this file tonight, and we can meet for breakfast in the morning."

He nodded. "Sounds like a good plan. Want me to check the room for you?"

"That's not necessary. Who would have known I would check in and get this room? I didn't even know until two minutes ago." Besides, she was perfectly capable of checking the room herself.

"Okay then. Have a good night. You have my number if you need anything." He pulled his cell phone from his pocket and flashed her a remorseful grin. "I grabbed it while we were at the cabin. Call me, and I promise I'll answer this time."

She spotted the multiple voice mail notifications the phone contained. They were probably all from her. He should feel bad for not responding to her for days. Oh well. The past was the past. He was making up for it now. "I'll see you in the morning."

She walked into her room and closed and locked the door behind her. It was a normal hotel room like any other she'd seen. A queen-size bed, TV, dresser, desk, nightstand and phone, along with a window overlooking the square below her third-floor room. She peeked out, glancing down at the street where she'd been nearly abducted yesterday. Her hands shook as she remembered the fear that had pulsed through her. She'd been to the deepest, darkest parts of the world without batting an eye, but an incident in small-town Texas had her hands trembling.

Someone had been watching her. That was the only explanation she could come up with for the latest attack.

Someone had followed her to Courtland. But who? And why? And how had she driven all this way without picking up on a tail? That was the question that bothered her the most. She was better trained than that.

She walked into the bathroom to splash water on her face and stared at herself in the mirror. Everything about this trip to Courtland had been surprising. She'd expected to see shock on Colby Avery's face at her resemblance to Tessa. What she hadn't expected was *her* reaction to *him*. The photograph in Tessa's office hadn't adequately conveyed his handsome features or the way her skin tingled when he touched her.

She flushed as she stared at herself in the mirror. "Are you seriously swooning over Tessa's boyfriend?"

She shook off those feelings. She was just tired and grief-stricken. She and Tessa had been as close as sisters once, but that relationship had deteriorated and they hadn't spoken in close to a year. Discovering her once beloved cousin had been murdered had rocked her world and had her questioning everything about her life. Only the need to find the man who had the answers she sought had driven her to get into the car and make the drive to Courtland. And that had turned out peachy.

She stepped out of the bathroom and immediately tensed. The balcony door stood open. Movement behind the door grabbed her attention. Before she could react, a hand pressed against her mouth, cutting off her ability to either breathe or scream for help.

THREE

"Where's the evidence Tessa collected?"

The hot, rancid feel of his breath on her neck sent shivers through her. Her heart hammered, and everything seemed to move in slow motion. This was the man who'd killed her cousin and attacked her twice before.

She only had a moment to think before she reacted, falling back on her training. She morphed into fight mode, ramming her head into his.

He cried out and his grip on her loosened. She grabbed the lamp from the nightstand and spun around, smashing it over his head. He cried out again as his knees buckled and he went down.

Brooke didn't wait to see if he got back up. She ran from the room, pulling open the door and running down the long hallway toward the elevators. Before she reached it, the door to another room opened.

Someone grabbed her arm. "What happened?"

Relief flooded her. She stared up into Colby's face. "Someone's in my room."

He pulled his gun from his holster and marched down the hall. She followed behind him.

"FBI! Freeze!" Colby shouted moments too late.

The intruder leaped off the balcony. They both ran for the open door and looked down to see him land on the balcony below and disappear into the room.

Colby rushed out, dashed down the steps and tried to follow him. Brooke locked herself inside the room instead of following. She dug through her bag for her gun. She would prefer to face her attacker armed if he returned.

She ran to the window but saw nothing outside and mentally kicked herself for not following Colby. Relief flooded her when a knock sounded on the door and she heard his voice. "Brooke, open up. It's me."

She turned the lock and let him inside.

"He got away. He darted down the stairwell before I could get to him." He pulled out his phone and pressed it to his ear. "Josh, get over here now. Someone attacked Brooke at the hotel."

She fell onto the bed, crossed her arms and tried to wipe away the chill that settled over her.

Colby knelt beside her. "Are you hurt?"

"I'm fine. Just shaken."

"I couldn't help but notice your intruder left a trail of blood behind him." He gave her a smile that said he was impressed with her ability to fight.

She'd been foolish not to grab her gun when she'd first arrived.

"Want to tell me what happened?"

"I came out of the bathroom and he grabbed me. I head-butted him and smashed the lamp over his head."

He glanced at the busted lamp on the floor and

flashed her an amused smile. "You're not much of a wilting flower, are you?"

"I was trained to protect myself." She'd acted on instincts instilled in her by the army and her training, but that didn't stop the shakiness of her hands or the feeling of dread that soared through her at recalling the assailant's demands.

"He wanted to know where Tessa hid the evidence she collected."

That got his attention. He turned and locked eyes with her. "The evidence?"

"You did say Tessa was collecting documentation."

"We never found it. I just assumed the killer had taken it."

"Well, I think you assumed wrong." She stood and glanced around at the mess in the room. Everything seemed to be falling apart.

Yet, when she looked at Colby, his blue eyes were shining with excitement. "This is good news. If that evidence she collected is still out there, it could lead us to her killer or whoever hired him."

It was true. If Tessa's evidence was out there somewhere, they had to find it before her killer did.

She glanced at Colby again.

Doubt had clouded his expression. "This is good news for the case, Brooke, but not for you. Whoever is behind this believes you know where that documentation is hidden. The question is how did they know about you in the first place?"

"I went to the hospital where she worked. I spoke

with people she knew. Is it possible I saw the killer there?"

"Tessa told me they often saw the Healthmax employees around the hospital. They have a separate facility, but it's attached to the hospital building through a back entrance. They don't even have to go outside to enter the hospital. One of them must have seen you there."

Everyone who'd seen her at Tessa's workplace had been shocked. She'd seen their stunned expressions as she'd walked through the hospital. She was certain she'd been the talk of the place that day. It wasn't a large facility. She was sure gossip spread quickly in such an environment. Anyone could have been alerted to her being there that day.

A knock on the door pulled their attention away from that concern. Colby's hand hovered over his gun in its holster. Brooke reached for her weapon and braced herself for conflict. But what kind of intruder knocked first?

"Who's there?" Colby asked.

"It's Josh."

She recognized his brother's voice and obviously he did too. His stance relaxed as he opened the door. Josh stood in the hallway along with several deputies.

"I'm glad you're here," Colby said.

Josh stepped inside and looked at her. "Are you hurt?" He had that same no-nonsense tone as Colby.

"I'm okay."

"But her intruder isn't," Colby told him. "He left a

trail of blood in the stairwell. She busted his nose and smashed this lamp over his head."

Josh turned to the deputies, issued instructions to collect any blood evidence they found and then turned back to them. "We'll collect anything we find and can use it as a comparison if we find the suspect. Maybe he left us some bloody fingerprints too." He looked at her, whistled admiringly, then shook his head and turned to his brother. "Guess she didn't need your protection after all, did she?"

Brooke turned to Colby and realized that was why he'd been in the room down the hall. "You rented a room on the same floor so you could keep an eye on me?"

He nodded but didn't appear contrite, which sent her hackles up. She wasn't some damsel in distress who needed his protection. "You didn't have to do that. I can take care of myself."

"Tessa thought she could too, but she's dead now."

His words were so real and so raw that they pained her. He didn't deserve her attitude, and she was thankful he'd been there tonight. "You're right. I'm sorry."

He seemed stunned by her apology and looked like he wanted to say something, probably something to do with Tessa, but he changed the subject instead. "This guy is not going to stop targeting you until we find him."

"Then we go to him. You said John Dutton was behind this. I say we go to that company and find the evidence we need." She'd been looking forward to confronting Dutton. Now seemed as good a time as any.

"I think a better idea is to find that documentation

Tessa collected. The man who attacked you wanted to know where it was. That means they don't have it. Let's trace Tessa's last steps and see if that leads us to the evidence. Then we use that to bring down her killers."

She'd had the same thought earlier but had no idea where to start looking. "I've been packing up her apartment. I started after I went to the police and they told me to contact the FBI. It took me a couple of days to get in to see your boss. I spent that time packing. I didn't see anything, but then again, I wasn't looking for evidence."

"It has to be there or at her office. I can't imagine where else she would have hidden it. We should also stop by the FBI offices and look through the evidence we bagged. Maybe we missed something."

She stared at him as he clicked through all the things that needed to be done. It was obvious what her cousin had seen in the handsome FBI agent. He was big and brawny, but he had a kindness in his eyes and a protective nature, a gentleness beneath his tough exterior that she was certain he only showed to a select few—Tessa, his family, and now her. He also carried a raw grief that was still evident even after all these months. Something about that softened her too. That connection, their shared loved for Tessa, was what bonded them together, as did their desire for justice.

"So, we're going to her apartment?"

He nodded, but she could see it was difficult for him to even think about going back there and sorting through her belongings. "We'll head to Dallas first thing tomorrow." He took a deep breath, his determination for justice greater than his grief. "God willing, we'll find what we need to end this."

She felt better having a plan. Together, they would find the evidence they needed to bring Tessa's killer to justice.

Why did he have to mention God?

Brooke stared in the rearview mirror at Colby's SUV following her as they headed back to Dallas. She was glad he was traveling with her, but why had he brought God into this? Even now, the next morning and a hundred miles away, his words still bothered her.

Tessa had been the one with the faith, not Brooke. God had never done anything for her or been present in her life. But Colby obviously believed. One more reason why she needed to get past her silly infatuation with her cousin's ex-boyfriend.

She remembered the photograph of Tessa and Colby and the love on her cousin's face for this man. She didn't want to trust him, didn't even want to like him, but she couldn't deny he was handsome. Tessa always did go for the handsome types. So did she.

Jack was handsome. Handsome and unreliable. A man who would do anything to complete the mission... even if it meant keeping her cousin's death from her. She couldn't let her mind go there. Colby wasn't Jack. She had to remember that Tessa had loved him. That had to be enough for her to trust him. With caution, of course.

Brooke needed to concentrate instead on finding the man who'd murdered her cousin and attacked her. Once he was in jail and they'd gotten justice for Tessa, she could be on her way, away from Colby Avery and the uncertainty he sparked inside her.

She'd spent a sleepless night reading through the FBI file Colby had given her. It had confirmed everything he'd told her about Tessa's murder, and she hadn't seen anything in it that gave her any new insight into the case.

She pulled into the apartment complex where Tessa had lived and parked in front of her building. Colby pulled his SUV into a parking space beside her. He hopped out and met her by the door. She couldn't miss the way his jaw tightened and muscles tensed as they walked toward the apartment. It looked like he was struggling with returning here and all the memories that probably invoked.

Brooke unlocked the door and stepped inside. Colby followed her and closed the door behind him. She watched his shoulders sag as he surveyed the room. A thousand memories flickered in his expression before he regained control.

"How long ago since you were last here?" she asked him.

"Months. Since before Tessa died."

Boxes littered the floor where she'd started to pack up some of Tessa's things. She hadn't gotten far. She certainly hadn't found anything that looked like it was connected to the fraud Tessa had uncovered. But then again, she hadn't been looking for anything like that.

"Might as well get started." He walked to the bookshelf. "She might have hidden the paper copies in a book, or they might be secreted on a flash drive or external hard drive. We can't be sure, so check everything. Journals, notes, drives."

She pulled open a box. Digging through Tessa's belongings the first time had been hard, but this time, slowing down and examining each item was brutal. Each held a memory of her cousin.

"When was the last time you spoke to her?" Colby must have seen how she was struggling, or maybe he was trying to keep his own mind off his emotions.

"Nearly eight months ago. We spoke on the phone briefly. It's been well over a year since we saw one another." She shook her head. That wasn't how family was supposed to behave. A tear slipped from her eye as she realized she would never get that chance again. "I should have been here for her."

"You had a demanding job. So did she. That's the way life is."

"You also have a demanding job, yet you find time to be with your family." She liked how he was with his brother. They seemed close.

His face reddened. "You found me in Courtland because I was hiding out. After losing Tessa and not being able to bring her killer to justice, I couldn't do my job any longer. The truth is that I hardly ever make it home unless someone is sick or in danger."

"In danger?" That seemed an odd thing to say. "How often does that happen?"

"More often than it should. I recently had to head to town to help protect my sister from someone who was trying to kill her and take her baby."

"That's awful."

"I managed to lead the bad guys right to where they were hiding. I should have known better. Thankfully, her boyfriend and my brothers were there. Together, we were able to find the baby and bring down the guy who was after her."

She could see that ordeal had taken a toll on him. He shouldered a lot of burdens. "I'm sure you did your best," she said.

"My best used to be better than that. I wasn't on top of my game after Tessa died, and I placed my sister's life in danger. That's when I finally decided to take a leave of absence from the FBI to clear my head."

Brooke understood not being able to focus. After learning about Tessa's death and Jack's betrayal, her attention to detail had taken a nosedive. She'd not only lost faith in Jack, but also in herself. She'd been glad to see the final days of her tour come to an end.

Now, both she and Colby needed to focus if they were going to figure out where Tessa had stashed the documentation that had gotten her killed.

She dug through a box of books she'd previously packed up but didn't find anything that might be a clue as to where Tessa had hidden the evidence. Two hours later, they'd been through all the boxes and cabinets and crevices in the apartment. They'd found nothing.

She stared at Colby and saw the same expression of frustration she must have worn. He ran a hand over his face and shook his head. "There's nothing here."

She had to agree. "What do we do now?"

"Let's head back to my office and go through the

physical evidence. Maybe we'll find some answers there. We'll take my car."

She locked up the apartment and followed him to his SUV. She was ready to take a look at the evidence and finally figure out who was behind all of this.

Colby drove to the FBI headquarters and parked in the garage. They stopped by the visitor's desk to obtain a badge for Brooke before heading to Greg's office. Colby shook hands with his boss. They'd gone through the academy together. He admired Greg. He was a good friend, and Colby couldn't have asked for a better supervisor.

Greg shook Brooke's hand as well and then motioned for them both to take a seat. "It's good to see you again."

"You too."

"I see you managed to track down Colby." He glanced over at Colby. "I imagine that was quite a shock."

"It was," Colby admitted. "Especially after she was nearly abducted right in front of me."

Greg's expression turned hard. He leaned forward. "Abducted? Maybe you'd better catch me up."

"A van appeared out of nowhere and shoved her inside. She managed to fight her way out." He took a chance and looked at Brooke. He'd come close to losing her too, another victim of his incompetence. No more. He was going to uncover who was responsible for these attacks and put a stop to it once and for all.

Colby handed over a file Josh and Cecile had put together from the attempts against Brooke. Greg glanced through it.

"This is all very troubling." He looked at Brooke. "Do you have someone who wants to hurt you?"

Colby answered instead. "We believe this has to do with Tessa. After the attempted abduction, someone attacked her at the hotel. He demanded to know where the evidence Tessa collected was."

Greg leaned back in his seat and steepled his fingers. "You believe this has something to do with the fraud investigation?"

"It must have. Somehow, someone must have seen Brooke when she came to town and mistakenly believed she was Tessa."

"How is that possible? Dallas isn't exactly a small town. We suspect someone at Healthmax is behind Tessa's death. How would anyone from there have seen her?" He turned to Brooke. "You didn't go there, did you?"

She shook her head. "I don't even know where Healthmax is, but I did go to the hospital where Tessa worked."

"It's possible she was seen there by someone at Healthmax. Their offices are right next door." Colby turned the conversation to the reason they'd come. "The guy who attacked Brooke wanted Tessa's evidence. We assumed the killer had taken it. However, it's possible Tessa hid it before she died. If we can find that—"

"It might lead you to her killer," Greg said, finishing his sentence. "That's a good idea. Let me know what you find out."

They stood and headed for the door. Before Colby could pass through it, Greg stopped him.

"I'm glad to see you're back, Colby."

Greg had given him a lot of leeway in this investigation. He'd lost his focus and his inspective will after Tessa's murder. "I want to bring her killer to justice, Greg. I believe Brooke can help me finally do that."

"I'm worried about you. I don't want to see this pull you under again."

He understood Greg's concern, but he couldn't—he wouldn't—give up on this case. Greg had threatened to hand it over to someone else multiple times. For all Colby knew, he did have someone else working on it. If Greg hadn't already moved the case to someone else, it wouldn't be long before he did.

Colby led Brooke to the evidence room. He pulled down three boxes of bagged evidence and carried them to a conference room table. He spread everything out, and they went through each item one by one. Her open wallet found at the scene, her ID and credit cards still inside. Clothes. Jewelry. Even the bandage from the cut on her hand. He was hoping something would spark with Brooke, but she looked as dumbfounded and pain-ridden as he did. He'd seen this all before. He was trained to look at physical evidence and try not to react. Even with his training, this was painful for him. It had to be devastating for Brooke. She'd said herself that it had been over a year since she'd seen Tessa, and months since they'd last spoken.

Her chin quivered as she set down a bagged shoe that had once belonged to her cousin and shook her head. "I can't— I don't know—"

He stopped her. "It's okay. It was a long shot anyway."

He could see this process was painful for her.

She sucked in a deep, fortifying breath. "No, I want to do this."

They took it slow as they searched through the bags of evidence but found nothing that might indicate where Tessa had hidden the documentation she'd collected. Defeated, they turned in Brooke's visitor's badge and left the building. At the SUV, she stopped and turned to him. "I want to go see Dutton."

"That's not a good idea," Colby said. He'd already lost Tessa to this investigation, and he didn't like the idea of putting her cousin in danger, especially a cousin who reminded him so much of Tessa. No, he had to remember Brooke was her own woman, strong and independent.

"I'm no frail flower," she insisted. "I worked undercover many times during my stint with army intelligence. I may not be a trained FBI agent, but I know what I'm doing."

"The FBI will never allow that," he insisted.

She jutted her chin and stared at him defiantly. "Then they don't have to know, do they?"

"You're putting me and Greg in a precarious situation."

"Look, Colby. I don't answer to you, and I don't answer to Greg. I'm going to that office building and confronting those people. Someone there is responsible for my cousin being dead."

He couldn't blame her. He also didn't see what good

it would do. "What do you hope to accomplish? Do you think the CEO is going to even see you, much less confess to you that he had Tessa murdered when he discovered what she was doing? They all know she's dead."

"That may be true, but there's one thing they don't know."

"What's that?"

"That she has a cousin who could be her identical twin."

"Seeing that they followed and attacked you multiple times, I'd say someone does know. What exactly is your plan?"

"I don't have one except to walk into that office and see what kind of reaction I can get out of everyone."

"Do you expect someone to burst out, 'Tessa, I thought I killed you,'" he said, using a fake voice.

"No, but seeing me—seeing her—has to elicit some kind of reaction."

"From almost anyone who knew her and knows she's dead."

"That's why I need you there too, Colby. I can't see everyone's reaction. You can see what I don't see, someone who isn't shocked to see me because they know I'm not Tessa."

"And what if they attack again?"

She locked eyes with him. "I'm counting on it."

He wasn't going to talk her out of this foolishness. She was intent on facing down these people to provoke a reaction from one of them. She was placing herself at risk, just like Tessa had done, only Brooke was already in danger. What harm could come to her in an office building in the middle of the day with him by her side?

"Fine. I'll come with you, but I don't have to like it."

They stopped at a store and she bought a pair of cheap glasses that matched the frames Tessa had worn. When she looked at him, his breath caught. She looked so much like Tessa that he momentarily forgot and had to fight the urge to pull her to him for a kiss. He wouldn't have had the right to do so anyway since Tessa had ended things between them, but their breakup hadn't meant his feelings for her had completely faded.

He found a spot in the hospital's parking garage and they got out. Healthmax took up an entire floor on the fifth level of the building adjacent to the hospital. They rode the elevator to the fifth floor.

Brooke was stiff beside him, tension flowing off her. Despite her reassurances that she'd worked undercover before, walking into these suites and confronting the man who'd likely had her cousin murdered and orchestrated attacks on her had to be taking its toll on her.

Colby's initial instinct was to take her hand and assure her that nothing was going to happen to her while she was by his side, but he checked that reflex. It not only made him seem like a Neanderthal, it would probably only fire her up even more. She'd already proven back at the hotel that she was no damsel in distress. She'd taken out her attacker even being ambushed and unarmed.

She could surely handle John Dutton.

The elevator dinged and the doors slid open. Colby stepped into the hallway. Brooke hesitated a moment or two then walked off and let the elevator doors close. He pulled open the main entrance door that had Healthmax stenciled on the glass. She might not be a damsel in distress, but his mother had taught him manners. He took out his cell phone and started recording. If they couldn't notice everyone's response, at least he could video it.

She walked to the receptionist's desk and greeted her warmly. The woman looked up, a pasted smile on her face. She stopped her greeting as her eyes widened. "Dr. Morgan?" Her mouth fell open and she gaped at Brooke for several confused, awkward pauses before she leaped from her chair and ran around it to pull Brooke into a hug. "I heard the rumors that someone saw you at the hospital a few days ago, but I didn't believe it. I can't believe you're alive." She spun around and announced to the room. "Everyone, look who it is."

Heads popped up from their desks, and Brooke smiled and waved at their wide-eyed, mouth-gaping responses. Several people jumped up and came over to greet her, all the while expressing their shock.

"I can't believe it," one woman stated. "I just can't believe it. The police said you died."

All their responses seemed genuine.

Colby took out his FBI credentials and showed them to the receptionist. "Tell Mr. Dutton we need to see him on an urgent matter."

She turned and walked back to her desk. After making the call, she pointed toward a row of chairs against the wall. "He'll be right down, Agent. If you'd please take a seat."

The crowd dispersed and Colby led Brooke to the

chairs. She was fidgety as they waited. He spotted her wipe away a stray tear. "You okay?"

She nodded and pushed a strand of hair from her face. "Everyone seemed genuinely surprised to see me. And relieved. They really did care for my cousin."

"She was easy to like. She made friends wherever she went."

Seeing people who'd cared for her cousin had shaken her. Colby reached for her hand and held it, meaning it as a reassuring gesture. She latched her fingers with his, and his heart skipped a beat, especially when she turned those probing green eyes his way. He held his breath. Something was definitely happening between them, but how could this strong, determined woman ever want anything to do with him after the way he'd gotten her cousin killed?

He heard John Dutton's voice before he saw him. "Agent, I thought we were done with this constant harassment."

Colby stood as the man approached. Dutton started to say something but stopped when he saw Brooke. His face paled and stunned surprise rolled over his expression. "Wh-what is this?"

"John Dutton, this is Brooke Moore. She's Tessa's cousin. We would like to ask you a few questions."

Dutton turned his attention back to Colby as he smoothed down his suit jacket and gathered his composure. "I've already told you everything I know about Dr. Morgan's death, Agent Avery. I have nothing more to say on that matter."

"How about the matter of someone trying to abduct

me twice in two days?" Brooke interrupted. She stood tall, firm, determined, as she confronted him.

He stared at her, his mouth agape. "I don't know what you're talking about." He turned back to Colby. "You're not going to try to rope me into something else, are you? I had nothing to do with Dr. Morgan's death and nothing to do with whatever attacks this woman is talking about."

Colby pulled his notebook and pen from his pocket. "Can you account for your whereabouts for the past two days, Mr. Dutton?"

"Everyone here can attest that I've been in the office working, and my wife will confirm that I was home the rest of the time. Now, if you have any further questions, you can contact my attorney." He gave Brooke one last look and then walked away, disappearing behind an office door.

That was it. It was over. They walked to the elevators and Colby pushed the button for the parking garage level.

"He certainly did seem surprised to see me," she said, and he couldn't argue with that. Dutton had been stunned when he'd laid eyes on her. If he'd known she was in town and had tried to abduct her, his surprise wouldn't have been so genuine. Colby didn't like the implications of that. Was it possible he'd been on the wrong trail this entire time?

They stepped onto the elevator and rode to the garage level. As they exited, Colby dug for his keys and pressed the fob to unlock his SUV.

The squeal of tires grabbed their attention. A van

roared around the curve, a figure leaning out of the passenger window. Colby spotted the barrel of a rifle.

"Get down!" he shouted, grabbing Brooke and pulling her to the ground.

Bullets sprayed the cars surrounding them.

FOUR

Colby grabbed his gun and leaped to his feet. Too late. The van was racing around the corner and out of sight.

Gone.

That didn't stop the hammering of his heart at yet another attack. He holstered his gun and glanced around. Bullet holes littered several vehicles around them. They'd taken cover just in time.

He hurried to Brooke. "Are you hit?"

She looked up at him. Fear clouded her green eyes. He helped her to her feet, holding her arms to steady her.

"I'm fine." Her trembling hands told a different story. "What do you think that was for?"

He glanced at the bullet-ridden cars surrounding them. "I guess we got someone's attention." It was an understatement at its best. The killer or killers had targeted her again.

He pulled out his phone and dialed for help. Greg arrived with an FBI forensics team just as an ambulance pulled in. They both had cuts and scrapes from the shattered car windows that had sprayed over them as they'd ducked for cover.

Brooke allowed the paramedics to bandage her scrapes. He was more focused on the scene.

"You could have both been killed," Greg said, his scowl indicating he wasn't happy with Colby. "Plus, you might have just opened a can of worms with legal over questioning Dutton. We were warned off."

He understood the pressure Greg had received from the legal department, but it couldn't be helped this time. "She was going with or without me."

Brooke walked over and gave Greg a hard stare. "This isn't Colby's fault. He was just trying to keep me safe."

He felt his face warm. He hadn't done such a good job with that. "Did anyone see the van that screeched out of here?"

Greg shook his head. "I've got the local police questioning bystanders, but there weren't many people in the garage at the time of the shooting. A few people standing outside the clinic across the street spotted it, but couldn't really give many details. We're pulling the security footage. They'll email it to the FBI offices."

Good. Colby was ready to get out of this place and back to office to try to figure out who had shot at them. That security feed was a good place to start. The two men in that van were probably the same people who'd targeted Brooke in Courtland. If they could identify them, they were on their way to wrapping this up.

Colby's SUV sported a cracked windshield, so he and Brooke hitched a ride to FBI headquarters with Greg. They stopped at the front desk long enough to get her a visitor's badge and then headed upstairs.

"I'm giving you complete access to conference room C, and I'll assign Olivia Mitchell to assist you."

Colby'd worked with Olivia previously. She was a good agent, and he was glad to have the assistance. "Thanks, Greg."

Greg stepped off the elevator and then stopped and turned to them. "Keep me updated with what you find." He walked down the hallway toward his office.

Colby steered Brooke in the opposite direction. "Conference room C is the last door on the left."

He pushed it open to find Olivia had already set up three laptops on the table and was connecting one wirelessly to the monitors mounted on the wall.

She stood when she saw them and reached out her hand. "It's good to be working with you on this again, Colby."

"You too. Olivia, this is Brooke Moore."

Olivia's eyes widened in surprise. She drew in a breath and shook Brooke's hand. "I heard about your resemblance to Dr. Morgan, but I didn't expect that you'd look just like her."

"It's nice to meet you." Brooke's tone showed no hint of annoyance, yet Colby saw the way her eyes crinkled at the mention of her resemblance to Tessa. The comparison was getting old.

"Have we received the surveillance video from the hospital yet?"

Olivia nodded, turned to one of the laptops and clicked a few keys. "Yes, it's here."

A grainy image popped up on one of the big screens on the wall, mirroring the picture on her laptop. Olivia moved the video forward until he and Brooke appeared in a corner of the screen. His muscles tightened. He should have been more alert of his surroundings. He'd been caught off guard.

Beside him, Brooke watched the footage, her arms folded and held close to her chest. Her breath hitched when the shooting started.

"You don't have to stay here and watch this. I can have someone take you home."

"You mean back to Tessa's apartment? No, I need to be here. I need to help with this investigation. Please don't push me out, Colby."

"I'm not trying to push you out, Brooke. I only thought you might need time to recuperate."

"I'll recuperate once these people who are targeting me are captured." She took in a deep breath and fortified herself before pointing at the screen. "Is there any way to identify the van?"

Olivia zeroed in on the tags of the van before responding. "The plates aren't visible. They've likely done something to obscure them. There's nothing special about it either. No logos or insignias that will help us identify it. We were able to track them leaving the parking garage through city traffic cams, but once they turned off on a corner street, they went out of our range."

"Then they could be anywhere?"

"Yes, but here's another thing I noticed." She replayed the image to the part where Colby shoved Brooke to the ground. "Did you see that? The shooter waited until Colby saw them and pushed you out of the way before he started firing."

Olivia was right. The shooter had hesitated. "Why would he do that?"

"It's possible they were shooting at you, Colby, but they didn't want to hit Brooke."

He saw where Olivia was going with this. "You think they wanted to abduct her?" After the multiple abduction attempts, it made as much sense as anything.

He turned to Brooke, who heaved a sigh and shook her head. "They think I can lead them to whatever evidence Tessa had. I can't."

"I believe you can. Why wouldn't they believe it too? But that means we have to make sure to keep you safe until we either find the evidence or until we capture whoever is calling the shots." He turned back to Olivia. "See if you can zero in on the driver. I'm almost certain the two people in that van were both men. Brooke, you said a man and a woman tried to abduct you in Courtland."

She nodded. "It was a woman's voice. I'm certain of it."

Olivia zoomed in as much as she could, but the angle of the camera wasn't great. Still, he thought he could make out facial hair on the driver's face. "It's hard to see, but I think that's a man."

That realization settled on Brooke's face. "Then we are dealing with more than two people?"

"At least two men and a woman. I'm going to send this information to my brother and have him verify if this is the same van used in the Courtland abduction attempt."

Brooke scoffed. "I wasn't aware the FBI shared information with small-town sheriffs."

"We do when it's necessary." Colby knew she'd worked in the intelligence community and was right that they didn't usually share information, but Josh was more than just a small-town sheriff. "I trust my brother's opinion and investigative skills more than I trust most people's."

Her face reddened. "Of course, you're right. I suppose I'm just used to agencies that guard their information with an iron fist."

She wasn't wrong about that.

He turned back to Olivia. "I want to do a deep dive on Dutton and the other Healthmax employees."

Olivia nodded. "I'll get started on that, but it's going to take some time. They have over a hundred employees."

He was anxious for answers, but it would take the three of them a long while to do those background checks. He wanted to hit Greg up for some more help but doubted his boss would approve it.

He glanced at his phone and saw a message from the forensics team. They'd finished collecting their data and were headed back to the office. From experience, he knew it would be a while before they finished their analysis and got those reports to him.

His stomach grumbled. They hadn't eaten in hours. Now was as good a time as any to run out for dinner before digging into those background checks.

"Why don't we get out of here and grab some food? There's a good diner right next door."

Brooke seemed pleased at the suggestion. "That sounds good."

"Are you sure you're okay to walk?" She was still limping slightly so he didn't want to push her.

She waved away his concerns. "I'm okay. It'll feel good to stretch my legs."

He nodded then turned to Olivia. "Bring you back something?"

She shook her head. "Thanks, but I brought something from home."

"Okay. We'll be back."

They walked downstairs to the main lobby and then outside. "The diner is just over here. A lot of cops and agents eat there so we should be safe." Despite his assurances, he still scanned the street for any possible threats.

"Sounds good."

A man bumped Brooke hard, sending her stumbling into Colby's arms. He held on to her, ignoring the way his heart skipped a beat at having her close enough to smell the scent of her lavender soap. He helped steady her and then searched out the man who'd disappeared into the crowd without even stopping to apologize. Rude people made his blood boil.

Brooke took his arm. "Forget it. It's fine. It's not worth it."

Irritation bit through him. He was supposed to be safeguarding her, but he couldn't even protect her from bad manners. He did his best to shake off the feeling, but it reminded him of how much he missed the open fields of the Silver Star. He'd gotten used to the lack of crowds and busy streets during his weeks at home.

Brooke stumbled again, and he reached out to help steady her. She gave him a small grin. "I seem to be all left feet today."

"It's understandable after what we've been through."

Her eyes widened and she stared up at him. She clutched his arms. "Something's wrong."

Her complexion paled, and her knees gave out. "I don't... I don't feel so good." He caught her, but she went limp in his arms.

He carefully lowered her to the ground. He touched her cheek. It was burning up. Her eyes rolled back in her head and her body began to shake. She was convulsing.

"Brooke? Brooke, can you hear me?"

No response.

He checked her pulse. It was rapid, and she'd started sweating. She was having some kind of reaction. But to what?

He took out his phone and called for an ambulance. His first instinct was to stop everyone in their path and cordon off the area until he could question them all, but that wasn't logical. He wasn't ready to leave her without knowing what was happening first.

He checked her over but found no obvious evidence of blood or a wound. He hadn't heard a gunshot either. But what else could have made her collapse?

After the ambulance, he dialed Greg's number and updated him.

"I'm on my way down, and I'm sending security," he said after Colby explained what had happened.

Colby spotted several uniformed officers hurry their way as a siren sounded blocks away. A crowd had gathered around them. Several people snapped pictures instead of stepping up to help.

It didn't matter. He wasn't letting anyone who wasn't official medical personnel near her. He checked her pulse again. It was out of control. Where was that ambulance?

Panic gripped him as all his guilt and shame over Tessa's death rushed back to him. This couldn't be happening. Not again.

He'd failed Brooke just as he'd failed Tessa.

Colby had hopped into the ambulance and ridden to the hospital with Brooke, his mind awhirl with questions about what had happened to her. One moment, she'd been fine. The next, seizing in his arms.

His phone rang as he sat in the waiting room where the nurses had instructed him to wait. "Any news?"

"Nothing yet. What did you find?"

"I've got the local police canvassing the area, but so far, no one saw anything. You were closest to her. You didn't see anyone?"

"There was a guy in a food delivery jacket who bumped into her as we came out of the building. I didn't see anything, but he must have done something." He rubbed the back of his neck. Until they knew what they were dealing with, there was little point in speculating.

A doctor appeared in the doorway and called his name. "I'll call you back." Colby ended his call and dashed toward him. "How is she? What happened?"

"She overdosed."

"Overdosed?" That didn't make any sense. "That's impossible."

"She had a large amount of methamphetamine in her system. We've treated her with Narcan, so she should be fine. She's also getting IV fluids, and we've hooked her up to a heart monitor. She'll need to be observed for a day or so."

Colby shook his head in disbelief. "I've been with her all day. How did she get meth in her system?"

"I noticed what looked like a needle mark on her hip during my examination. If, as you say, you've been with her all day and don't believe she injected the drug herself—"

"She didn't," Colby insisted. "She was fine when we left for lunch."

"I believe you. She doesn't have any obvious signs of a meth addiction. Someone could've injected her with it. She might not even have realized it was happening."

The delivery guy who'd bumped into her on the sidewalk. It had to be him. No one else had gotten close enough. No wonder he hadn't stopped to make sure she was okay. He'd known she wasn't.

"How long after it was injected would this have an effect?"

"Not long at all. A few minutes at most. She's resting now. I'll let you know when you can see her."

He thanked the doctor and pulled out his cell phone to call Olivia. "Pull the security footage from in front of the building for minutes after Brooke and I left you. I'm looking for a food deliveryman. He had dark hair under a ball cap, and he was wearing a black jacket. He bumped into Brooke just after we left the building. I believe he injected her with something."

"Greg already told me. I'll go through them the moment I receive them," Olivia stated. "How is she doing?"

"The doctor says she's going to be fine. I'm waiting to see her now. Let me know what you find on that footage."

"Will do."

He breathed out a weary sigh and fell into a chair. None of this made sense. The attackers had to know a dose of Narcan would reverse the effects of an overdose. So why would they go to these lengths to inject her with something?

The nurse came through and waved to him. "You can see her now."

He followed her down the hall to a room. Brooke was lying in the bed, looking drained of every ounce of energy.

"How do you feel?" he asked.

Her eyes were glassy, but she smiled up at him. "Tired. What happened?"

"It looks like someone injected you with something."

She thought about it. "That guy that bumped into me. I thought he'd pinched me, but he stuck me with a needle, didn't he?"

"Probably. I've got Olivia pulling the security surveillance now. You just rest. Everything is going to be okay."

"I don't get it. Why inject me? Have they decided I'm

not worth abducting? Are they changing tactics? Now they want to kill me?"

"I don't have the answers, but we'll find them. Together." He reached instinctively for her hand before he realized what he was doing. Instead of pulling away, she held it.

He sucked in a breath, amazed by the feel of her skin on his. Brooke's hands were strong and soft, very different from the feel of Tessa's petite grip. No one who'd ever held them both would mistake Brooke for her cousin.

She drifted off to sleep, and Colby stretched out on the small couch in the room. It was short and uncomfortable, but it would have to do. He wasn't leaving her side.

He must have dozed off, because an alarm awoke him.

Overhead, the hospital intercom sounded. *"Code Black. Code White. All sections."*

Code Black? That meant a bomb threat on the premises.

He jumped to his feet. Surely, he'd heard wrong.

Brooke pushed up in the bed. "What is it? What's wrong?"

"I'll find out." He pulled open the door and spotted nurses and orderlies scrambling. He grabbed an arm as one of them passed by him. "What's happening?"

"No need to panic, sir, but we're evacuating the hospital. Someone will be in to get you in a few minutes."

He pulled out his FBI credentials and showed them to her. "Has the threat been verified?"

The nurse's eyes widened at the question. "I—I don't know. All I know is we got the alert."

He glanced at his cell phone. No bars. They were jamming cell phone signals. Not good. He strode to the nurses' station and grabbed the landline, intent on dialing security for an update, but before he could, a man in a uniform pushed open the door.

"I'm with hospital security. I'm in charge of overseeing the evacuation of this floor."

Colby pulled out and showed his credentials. "What's going on?"

He glanced at the credentials and was apparently satisfied. "We received a suspicious call about a bomb placed in the building. We were able to substantiate it, so we've alerted local police and are starting evacuation procedures."

"What did the threat say specifically?"

"That a bomb had been placed inside a backpack and left in one of heating vents of the hospital. We have video surveillance of a man wearing a backpack entering the hospital and images of him leaving twenty minutes later without it."

"Did the caller give a reason for this attack?"

"He said he was striking a blow against government-funded healthcare. Why are you here? Do you have someone here who might be the intended target?"

He did. And he was certain Brooke was the target of all this. It would be an enormous coincidence if she wasn't.

The man glanced around him as nurses and orderlies began moving people from their rooms. "Agent, I need to oversee the evacuation of this floor. Will you help me?"

Colby wasn't leaving Brooke unprotected and alone for long in case this was a trap meant for her. But he couldn't sit back and ignore this threat to others either.

He grabbed a wheelchair and hurried into Brooke's room. "We have to go. They're evacuating the hospital."

She pushed back the blankets, and he helped her into the wheelchair. "What's happening?"

"Someone called in a bomb threat. I'm going to help security with the evacuation, but I don't want you going with anyone but me. If anyone tries to take you out of here, give a holler."

He pushed her to the nurses' desk where he could keep an eye on her. He could see she longed to get up and help but was too weak from the drugs. He worked with the nurses to hurry everyone they could into the service elevators. They were safer taking the stairs, but getting patients down safely would be difficult with the necessary use of wheelchairs.

He hurried back to Brooke and clicked off the chair's locks. The elevator cars had gone, but they would take the next one. He would carry her down if he had to.

He wished for some way to contact Greg or someone in charge to get an update, but he had nothing. The alarms continued to sound as the floor cleared out.

A man dressed in scrubs burst through the stairwell door. He poked his head into several rooms just to be sure they'd been cleared out. "Are you the last?"

"Yes, I think we are. Everyone else has been evacuated."

"Good. Good."

Colby pressed the button to the cargo elevator and watched as the numbers led up to the sixth floor. When the light on the screen hit five, the man turned and round-kicked Colby, sending him backward into the counter of the nurses' station.

Pain radiated through his head. He reached for his gun, but the man hovered over him then hit Colby with something hard. He didn't know what. That blow sent him sprawling to the floor, unable to move. He did his best to push himself up, but his arms wouldn't work, and his head felt heavy.

All he saw before the darkness pulled him under was the man pushing Brooke onto the elevator, her eyes wide with fear as the doors closed.

FIVE

Pain was the first thing Colby knew as consciousness pulled him back. He didn't know how long he'd been out, but his mind immediately went to Brooke. He crawled to his feet, his head pounding and stars dancing around his vision.

He stared at the closed elevator doors. Brooke was gone.

His gun lay on the floor. Odd that the attacker hadn't taken it. He must have had one of his own. He scooped it up and holstered it, his head swimming in response to bending down to get it. The assailant had knocked him out good. He was still feeling the effects but had no time to wait for his head to clear. Not with Brooke's life in danger.

His cell still had no signal. He picked up the phone on the desk and dialed the number taped to the phone for the security office. "This is Agent Colby Avery with the FBI. We have an abduction from the sixth floor. I need all the exits blocked."

"Sorry, but all our resources are working on the evacuation. You should get out too. We've got the bomb squad on the way."

He slammed down the phone. They were going to be no help at all. They were only doing their jobs, but finding Brooke was his top priority. He hurried toward the stairwell. He suspected the bomb threat had been a ploy to get to her but he couldn't be certain.

Colby burst into the lobby where people were exiting the building. All around him, folks were checking their phones and shaking their heads. No calls were getting through. Still blocked. He needed to get far enough away to where his signal could go through, but he wasn't leaving this property. Not without her.

He searched through the crowd but saw no indication of Brooke or the man who'd taken her. A security guard tried to stop him when he left the crowd. Colby ignored him and circled the building. Multiple entrances had people hurrying through but there was no sign of Brooke anywhere.

Above the murmur of the crowd, a scream pierced the air. He bolted toward the sound and found Brooke. Her kidnapper had one arm wrapped around her neck and was dragging her toward the loading dock. She was struggling against him the entire way.

Colby drew his weapon and rushed toward them. "FBI! Let her go!"

He couldn't safely fire his weapon with all these people around, but the assailant must not have known that. He shoved Brooke down a flight of concrete stairs off the breezeway and took off running, disappearing into the crowd.

Colby didn't pursue him. He put his gun away and hurried to Brooke. She'd landed at the bottom of the stairs but was somehow still conscious. Barely.

"It's okay, Brooke. I'm here."

A woman in scrubs came running and knelt beside him. "I saw what happened. Is she okay?"

"I don't know."

The woman examined each of Brooke's extremities and checked her eyes. "I don't think anything is broken, but we need to move her away from the building. I'll go find a gurney."

"Don't bother."

He scooped Brooke up into his arms and ran toward the parking lot. He doubted there was a bomb, figured it had merely been a ruse to get to Brooke, but he couldn't take any chances. He wouldn't take any more risks with her life.

Once they reached the safe zone, he gently placed her on the ground. She was barely conscious but smiled when he looked down at her. "You're going to be okay, Brooke. I'm here. You're going to be fine."

He stared around at the people gathered outside the hospital. It had been a massive undertaking to clear out the hospital. If this had been a ruse, it was an elaborate one—all for one woman's possible abduction.

"Colby." Brooke tried to sit up, but he pressed her to remain still.

"I'm okay," she said, trying to reassure him. "I'm not hurt."

"Still, I'd rather you stay put until someone can examine you." Colby looked up and spotted Greg heading their way. "I'll be right back," he told her. He got up and walked to meet him.

"How is she?" Greg asked.

"She's tough. Thankfully, there are no broken bones, but she hit her head. Plus, she's still weak from the drugs they injected into her. She needs rest." He looked around at the chaotic scene. "I doubt she'll get any here anytime soon."

"We just received word that the bomb squad has completed their search. They found the backpack but it was loaded with plastic bags stuffed inside. No evidence of any kind of explosive. Our technical team is working with the local police to see if we can identify where the call came in."

"I want to remain here with Brooke, if that's okay. Keep my eye on her."

"Of course." Greg patted him on the back and walked off, shouting orders into his phone.

Colby didn't envy Greg his responsibility. Having one person's life on his shoulders was enough for him. He grabbed a bottle of water from a cooler that had been provided, along with a couple of packs of chips and returned to Brooke, who was sitting on the ground atop a blanket that had been laid out for her. Everyone was just waiting for the all-clear to return to the hospital.

He sat beside her and handed her the water and chips. "Feeling any better?"

She opened the water and took several gulps before answering him. "Physically, I'm sore and tired. Emotionally, I'm outraged. That man grabbed me, and I couldn't do anything to fight him off."

"I think that was by design, Brooke. They wanted you weak." He shot her a smile. "After the way you clocked that guy in the hotel room in Courtland, I can't say I blame them for taking precautions."

He was trying to lighten her mood, and it seemed to help. She gave him a small smile and then sighed. "I hate feeling so helpless." Tears flooded her eyes. "I wonder if that's how Tessa felt when she was killed."

Hearing Tessa's name reminded him of his failure. He'd lost her, and he'd nearly lost Brooke today. Out of the hundreds of people who'd been evacuated, how had he found her? He still didn't know, but he was thankful he had.

After several hours, they were finally allowed back inside. Brooke returned to her hospital bed, and the rest of the night was uneventful. She fell asleep quickly and rested through the night while Colby camped out on the makeshift sofa with his legs hanging over the edge.

He awoke in the morning and headed to the cafeteria for coffee after posting a security guard at her door. The flow of the hospital was back on track and everything seemed normal to him. But whoever was after Brooke was still out there, waiting and watching.

He headed for the elevator, pressed the button, and was waiting when he spotted Greg approaching.

"I was just coming up to see you. We need to talk." Greg's tone was serious. He led Colby back into the cafeteria and they took a seat. Colby took the file Greg handed him, opened it, and his eyes went wide at the picture inside.

"This is the same guy who grabbed Brooke yesterday. Do we know who he is?"

"His name is Timothy Mason. We've issued a BOLO for him and sent it to all law enforcement agencies in the state and the neighboring states."

"What connection does he have to the fraud that Tessa suspected?"

"There's no record of him working for Healthmax or anywhere near this facility. His last known place of employment was an air-conditioning company. They haven't seen him since the beginning of the week. He didn't show up for work and didn't call in." He leaned back in his chair, his face grim.

"What are you not telling me, Greg?"

"Are you sure this is the man who tried to abduct Brooke."

"I'm positive. I got a good look at him, right down to the tattoo on his neck. Why?"

"Surveillance cameras got a good image of him too, and we ran his image through our facial recognition. It just doesn't make any sense."

"Why? Who is he?"

Greg's demeanor was troubling. Whoever this guy was, it was bad news.

"He has a long criminal record for assault and weapons charges, but most recently, he's been associated with a group of radical extremists with grudges against the government. They call themselves the FGI—Freedom from Government Interference. Our terrorist unit recently identified them as a growing threat."

Colby leaned back in his chair and took in that news.

Brooke had a group of anti-government radical extremists after her? That didn't make any sense. "But the guy who attacked her at the hotel specifically asked her about the files Tessa collected. What does a homegrown terrorist organization have to do with a healthcare fraud ring?"

"We don't have those answers yet, but we're working on them. I advised Matt Mercer of the Joint Terrorism Task Force to do a deep dive into this organization. Unless we find another explanation, there has to be a connection. Show her Mason's photograph and see if she recognizes him from somewhere else beside the abductions. Maybe she can shed some light on this."

Colby gathered the files and headed back upstairs. None of this made any sense to him. Why would an extremist group target Brooke, and what did they have to do with Tessa's murder? There had to be a connection they were missing.

Brooke's jaw tensed when he showed her the photo of Timothy Mason. "That's him. That's the man who tried to abduct me."

"I recognized him too. They pulled this image from the hospital security surveillance. Greg believes he called in the bomb threat to clear the hospital so he could abduct you in the chaos."

"He nearly succeeded." She pushed the photo away. "What does he want with me?"

"He has ties to an anti-government extremist organization. Is it possible whatever you were working on with army intelligence ties into this?"

She shook her head and pushed the image away, but

her body went tense. "No. All of my missions were overseas. They had no connection to homegrown terrorism."

She lowered her head and swallowed hard, clear indications she was hiding something from him. Something classified that she couldn't talk about maybe. "Are you sure? Maybe we should contact your commander just to be certain there isn't some link you're not aware of."

"Most of my work was classified, so I doubt my commander would have anything to tell you. Besides, I know what I worked on, Colby, and it had nothing to do with this. Are you forgetting the man who attacked me at the hotel wanted whatever it was Tessa had? I know she didn't have any connections to terrorist organizations, homegrown or otherwise."

He rubbed his chin, frustrated at the lack of answers. It was like they'd hit a brick wall. "I know, I know."

"Maybe this Mason guy is just a hired gun. You know, whoever is behind Tessa's death hired him to do their dirty work."

"It's possible, but if you've killed one person already, why would you need to hire someone to do that kind of work for you?"

"I don't know. I'm just trying to come up with answers."

"Me too."

He put away the photographs and the file and fell into a chair beside her bed. "You look better today."

"I'm sore. Thankfully, nothing was broken. It could have been worse."

He cleared his throat. Time to admit he'd failed her.

"I'm sorry I wasn't able to stop him from getting to you."

"You have nothing to be sorry for, Colby. You saved my life."

Yes, he'd been able to save her, but what about Tessa. Why could he save Brooke but not her? He stared into Brooke's lovely green eyes and felt a tug on his heart. Recalling the look on her face when those elevator doors had closed still stabbed him. It shouldn't have gone that far. He shouldn't have allowed it.

Failure was all he saw when he looked at her. Failure to keep her cousin safe, and failure to keep her out of the hands of a killer.

"I need to go to the office and follow up with Greg about the bomb threat and this Timothy Mason fella. I'll arrange to have a security officer guard your door. You'll be safe until I get back."

She nodded. "I'll be fine. And, Colby, you need to get some rest too."

He nodded, picked up the folder and left. He wanted to remain, didn't want to leave her side, but he wasn't going to solve this case from her hospital room. He needed to get to FBI headquarters and figure this out.

How did terrorism and healthcare fraud intersect into abduction and murder?

Brooke watched Colby walk out. It would be hours before she saw him again, and something about that made her sad. She was way too attached to the handsome FBI agent her cousin had fallen in love with. Way too close.

And why had she gotten so defensive when Colby wanted to contact Jack? Her tone had been uncalled for because he was right to ask about her work and make certain it had nothing to do with what was going on. She was sure it didn't, but would it have hurt to verify that?

It would mean speaking to Jack again, and that wasn't something she was up for. Neither did she look forward to what Jack might tell Colby if he called. She certainly couldn't trust Jack to keep it professional. Would he try to assert his possessiveness over her and give Colby the wrong idea about their relationship? And what exactly was the right idea? She wasn't Jack's girlfriend any longer, but she also wasn't available to be Colby's, no matter how much her growing attraction to him said otherwise.

She covered her eyes with her forearm and tried to stop the merry-go-round of thoughts and emotions that had taken over her brain. She hadn't come here for romance, and it didn't matter what she thought about Colby. Men couldn't be relied upon. Even Tessa had broken up with him, so how reliable could Colby really be? Sure, he'd given her that excuse about his job being too dangerous, but Brooke couldn't imagine such a thing causing anyone to end a relationship.

She glanced at her cell phone on the bedside table and heaved a sigh. She knew what she had to do. She picked it up and dialed Jack's number.

"Brooke, sweetheart. It's good to hear from you. I've tried calling several times, but you haven't answered my calls. How are you?"

Tears sprang to her eyes at his smooth, soothing

voice. She'd loved him so much, and he'd ripped out her heart. "I'm in trouble, Jack."

His tone instantly changed to serious concern. "Where are you? What's the matter?"

"I'm still in Dallas. I've been looking into my cousin's murder. Only now, the killer is after me."

"Why?"

"Tessa hid some information before she died. They seem to believe I can lead them to it."

"Brooke, come home. Get on a plane now. They won't follow you here, and if they do, I'll take care of them."

She shook her head even though she knew he couldn't see it. It was more to reinforce her determination. She didn't need Jack to be her knight in shining armor. She didn't need any man for that. "I'm not leaving, not until I have the answers I came for. Even then, I'm not returning to the army. I thought I had made myself clear."

"I get it. You're still mad at me. I've already apologized. I don't know what else you expect me to do."

"There's a difference between saying you're sorry and actually being sorry, Jack. You're only sorry that you got caught. Even if I could forgive you for your infidelity, I could never forgive how you kept Tessa's death from me."

"Brooke, there was nothing you could have done for her."

"I missed her funeral. I could have been there."

He gave a weary sigh. "Did you want something or did you just call to chew me out over the same things again?"

She hated how belligerent he got when things weren't going his way. "We've identified the man who tried to abduct me. His name is Timothy Mason, and he has ties to an extremist group operating here in the States. I want to make sure he doesn't have anything to do with something we worked on."

"'We've identified'? Who is 'we'?"

"I'm working with the FBI on my cousin's case. They believe it might be connected to healthcare fraud, but then this guy popped up. Have you ever heard his name?"

"No, I haven't. Let me do a quick data search for the name." She heard him tap the keys on his laptop. "Nothing is popping up. It doesn't look like he has any connections to cases we've worked."

That was good to know. At least she could tell Colby she'd crossed that off the list. "Okay, thanks, Jack." She started to end the call but Jack's voice stopped her.

"Wait, Brooke. I am sorry."

She didn't wait to hear more. She disconnected and fought back her anger. She'd loved Jack so much, but his betrayal had nearly destroyed her. It had destroyed her ability to trust anyone. How could you claim to love someone so much and then hurt them so badly?

She put away the phone and sank into the sheets on the bed. She was no closer to finding Tessa's killer, but she was one step closer to joining her cousin if she didn't find what these people were after.

Colby picked Brooke up from the hospital the next evening and drove her to Tessa's apartment. He'd spent all day yesterday and most of today at the office, checking on her periodically by phone, for which she was grateful. She'd done her best to rest, though it hadn't been easy. She was weak and sore, but she hated not being included in the investigation. He'd told her he needed her to help solve the case. He'd better not be trying to push her out now.

So when he went through two traffic lights without mentioning the case, she was ready to dig into him. "What have you discovered?"

Colby fidgeted in his seat and, for a moment, he looked like he wasn't going to answer her. She shot him a stare, daring him not to be honest with her. Finally, he sighed. "Not much. We ran Mason's name through our files. He's a known associate of a radicalized anti-government group called the Freedom from Government Interference—FGI for short. They've mostly organized protests and rallies in front of government buildings to advocate for less government control, but there have been murmurings in ATF and Homeland Security that the group has started stockpiling weapons and explosives. Our terrorism task chief believes they have a new leader who is radicalizing the group."

Hate groups weren't anything new, but they didn't generally target civilians who had no government ties. "Have you discovered any connection between them and Tessa? Or me?"

"No. The truth is that we don't have much information about Mason period, not even a current address. A warrant for his arrest has been issued and is being circulated, but who knows if and when he'll be apprehended. So far, we can't tie Dutton to him either. There's nothing in his background or financials to suggest any connection to this group."

"There might not be if he's using illegal means to hide his involvement. They must be using the money they're making from the healthcare fraud scheme to fund their anti-government activities. That's the only thing that makes sense."

"I agree. Now, if only we could prove it."

Proof. Tessa had had proof. Now she was dead. "I guess that explains their intense desire to find that documentation. If their fraud is exposed, so is their organization before it even gets off the ground."

Brooke shuddered as a chill ran up her spine. She wasn't used to being targeted. She was used to operating in the shadows. It was an eerie feeling to know someone was watching her.

He parked in front of Tessa's building, but neither of them moved to get out. She wasn't thrilled about going back into that apartment. There were too many memories of Tessa there. It should give her comfort to be surrounded by her cousin's belongings. It should, but it didn't, not after the way she'd allowed their relationship to deteriorate. Colby wasn't the only one with a guilty conscience.

She sucked in a breath, opened the door and got out. Colby followed, walking with her to the front door. Her hands shook as she reached for the key, and he covered her hand with his.

She glanced up into his face. He had kind eyes, full of understanding and empathy. He knew what she was going through. He'd been through it too, and their shared guilt and grief for Tessa connected them, as did her killer.

He unlocked the door and pushed it open, then he drew his gun. "Let me check it out first."

She could do it, but her gun was stashed in a bag inside the apartment, and she wasn't exactly feeling up to it at the moment. She watched him move from room to room and then return to the den and holster his gun. "Everything's clear." He placed the keys on the counter but didn't move to leave. "You should get some rest. I'll check on you in the morning. I'll bring you breakfast."

She liked the idea of breakfast…and of seeing him again despite her misgivings. "I've been doing nothing but rest. I'm not sure I'll be able to sleep tonight. Especially not here."

Boxes were still stacked in the corner, and they'd unboxed most of what she'd packed. At least she had something to do if sleep wouldn't come.

"I'll be fine."

"I'm having a patrol officer stationed outside to keep an eye out. I'll remain until he arrives." He moved to the door and opened it. "Good night, Brooke."

"Good night."

She locked the door once he was gone and dug through her suitcase and found her 9 mm. At least she didn't have to worry about defending herself. Anyone who tried to break in tonight would be in for a big surprise. She lay down but, as she'd suspected, sleep wouldn't come. After hours of tossing and turning, she crawled out of bed.

Colby's SUV was gone when she peered out the front window. A patrol car sat in its place. The morning sun was just starting to peek out above the horizon.

She scanned the apartment complex. It wasn't much different than a hundred she'd seen before. It was all concrete and buildings and cars. Her mind went to the beauty of the Silver Star Ranch and how lovely the sunrise would look over that horizon. That would be like a dream come true.

Only, in her dreamworld, no one got murdered.

Brooke gathered up a stack of books and loaded them into a box. Sitting around thinking about how her life should have turned out would do her no good. She had work to do, and it was better than letting her mind wander to places it shouldn't…places like Colby Avery.

How could she be having such strong emotions for the man her cousin had loved? She'd never seen Tessa in love, but that photo, the happiness on her expression at the moment the photo had been captured, spoke volumes. She'd loved Colby. Brooke didn't know why it hadn't worked out between them, except for the excuse Colby had given her about his job being too dangerous. If her own experiences were any indication, she could guess what the problem could've been.

Men let her down. All men had let her down. Right up from the first male figure—God. Okay, so maybe He wasn't a man, but where was He in all of this? Where was He when Brooke had been desperate and alone? When Tessa was being murdered? Her cousin had been a believer since they were teenagers and attended youth group at a local church. For Brooke, it had been a fun place to go and hang out, but her cousin had taken it seriously. She'd believed.

Where are You, God?

Her phone rang, startling her out of her reverie. She walked to the counter to grab it and glanced at the screen. Jack. She didn't want to pick up their conversation where they'd left off yesterday. He was probably calling to apologize, but she was in no mood to listen to his excuses for his behavior. She'd heard them all, and none of them made up for the fact that he'd let her down too many times.

While she was trying to gather her courage to ignore his call, another call came through. This one made her smile. Colby. She hit the answer button and said hello, but that was all she managed to get out.

Something rocketed through the glass in the front window and shattered against the floor. Flames erupted on the carpet and attacked the walls. A Molotov cocktail.

"Brooke! What's happening?"

She heard the panic in Colby's voice through the phone, yet couldn't catch her breath long enough to respond.

She covered her mouth, but not in time. The air choked her when she tried to take in a breath. She doubled over in a coughing fit. The scent of gasoline filled the room, energizing the hot, roaring flames.

She had to get out of the apartment before it was too late. She turned in the direction of the door. The flames had spread to that wall and engulfed the carpet around it, blocking her exit. She ran to the bathroom,

wet a towel and placed it over her face to try to deter
the thick, black smoke filling the apartment and burning her eyes.

Brooke followed the wall toward the bedroom and
tried to find the window, but she was all turned around.
This wasn't her apartment, and she couldn't see anything. The plumes blocked her vision and the towel
wasn't thick enough to filter out the smoke. She couldn't
see. She couldn't breathe. And she was trapped inside
a burning building.

She was in trouble.

Her knees buckled, but she kept crawling. She didn't
know which direction she was headed in or if she was
close to the window. It was amazing how quickly she'd
become disoriented in the small, unfamiliar apartment.

Sirens wailed, and she hoped they were for her.
Hoped someone would come help her.

She gasped for air and choked on the heavy black
smoke instead. This couldn't be it. This couldn't be how
she died. She hadn't even found Tessa's killer yet. Now,
he would be responsible for two deaths.

The door burst open, and a light shined through it. A
figure rushed toward her, scooped her up in his strong
arms and carried her like a rag doll toward the light.
She knew who it was the moment he lifted her into his
arms. Colby. He'd burst into a burning apartment to rescue her. She leaned into him, safe in his arms.

She felt the difference the moment they reached the
doorway. Crisp, cool air flowed over her, a welcomed
change from the burning heat of the fire. And air, sweet

air, surrounded her. She tried to breathe but gasped again.

"Careful," Colby told her. "You've probably inhaled too much smoke. The ambulance is on its way. They'll have oxygen."

He placed her on the grass and she didn't try to move. All she cared about was that they were both safe. Colby had taken a huge risk coming for her, but he'd rescued her from certain death.

He knelt beside her and she stared up at him. His face and arms were covered in soot. She followed his gaze to the roaring fire that was Tessa's apartment. All of Tessa's belongings were inside. Everything that had been her cousin's life gone, along with all her own belongings. Up in smoke in a heartbeat. Had that been the plan? Burn up any clue to where Tessa might have hidden her documentation. Oh, and kill Brooke too in the process?

"How—" She gulped at the raw gruffness of her throat when she tried to speak. "How did you know?"

She'd answered his call, but how could he have gotten here in time?

"I was down the road. I was coming to bring you breakfast like we talked about, and relieve the patrol."

The patrol officer on duty. Where had he been when someone had gotten close enough to toss a firebomb through her window. "Where is he?"

Colby's grim look told her all she needed to know. "Dead. Had his throat slashed while he sat in the car."

Anguish washed over her and the tears caused by the

burning smoke mingled with tears of frustration and sadness. These men were ruthless.

The paramedics arrived and placed her on a gurney. They administered oxygen and bandaged burns she hadn't realized she'd gotten. Now, they stung like crazy. She watched as the firefighters battled the blaze in Tessa's apartment while evacuating others who might be affected.

Brooke had nearly died inside that apartment, unable to get out on her own. She again owed her life to Colby. As she watched the flames destroy the last of everything her cousin had owned, she realized the truth.

No one had tried to abduct her. This time, her assailants hadn't bothered with kidnapping. They'd obviously decided killing her was a much better idea.

Everything had just changed.

SIX

Colby wiped soot from his face as he walked toward the ambulance where Brooke was being treated. His heart was still pounding, and his ears were burning from the chewing out the fire chief had given him. He'd made a foolish choice entering that building, but he couldn't wait, could he? Not knowing that Brooke was inside.

He'd nearly had a heart attack when he'd heard the glass shattering and her screams before the phone went dead.

Thank You, Lord, for letting me be close by when this happened.

"Agent Avery, you need oxygen too," a paramedic told him.

He sat on the bumper of the ambulance and allowed himself to breathe in the fresh, clean air. His throat and lungs were burning, but so was his anger. The chief had insisted they had to wait until they had all the facts, but no one had to tell him this fire had been intentionally set. The black smoke and smell of gasoline were all the proof he needed. There was no way that fire had spread as fast as it had without some kind of accelerant. Everyone within a two-mile radius could probably smell it.

"We're taking Brooke to the hospital," the paramedic told him, causing his heart to immediately kick up a notch.

"Is she okay?"

"She's fine, but she needs to be observed for a while. It looks like she inhaled a lot of smoke." He glanced around and then turned back to Colby. "I know the chief told you that you shouldn't have gone inside, but you saved that woman's life tonight. She wouldn't have survived another few minutes."

He thanked the paramedic. Yes, he'd rescued Brooke, but he wouldn't have had to rescue her if he'd put Tessa's killer away to begin with. He didn't know how he was going to prove that Dutton was behind this, but he had to.

His phone buzzed and he saw it was his brother, Josh. "Hello," he said, answering the call.

"Hey, wha—" He stopped midsentence. "Are those sirens I hear? What's going on?"

"Tessa's apartment is on fire. Brooke got trapped inside, but I managed to get her out."

"Are you okay? Are you hurt?"

"Just a little smoke inhalation. They've got me on oxygen now."

"Have you been to the hospital?"

"Not yet. They just transported Brooke, but I want to stick around and wait for the final confirmation that this fire was intentionally set."

"You think she was targeted again?"

"I'm certain of it. One minute, she was talking to me, the next, everything was chaos."

"I'm glad you're safe. Call me later when you have some answers."

"Did you want anything specific?" Colby asked him.

"It's not that important. It can wait." He paused for a moment and then continued. "I think you should think about bringing Brooke back to Courtland. We can keep her safe here."

"I don't know if she'll be up for that, but I think it's a good idea. I'll talk to her about it."

He ended the call with Josh. He thought his brother was right. Leaving Dallas might help to keep her safe, especially if they could sneak out when no one was watching. Of course, it didn't help that the killer had already followed her to Courtland once, but that didn't mean he knew where the Silver Star was located.

God, please help me keep her safe.

He couldn't lose anyone else.

By the time the fire was extinguished, a crowd of residents and onlookers had gathered in the parking lot. The building was surrounded by police, rescue personnel and fire trucks. The chief walked over to him and nodded. "I'm definitely classifying this as arson."

No kidding. At least he wasn't hedging around the classification. That was something.

Colby reached into his pocket and handed him a business card. "This card has my email on it. Once you complete your report, I would appreciate a copy of it sent to that address. We believe this incident has to do with an ongoing FBI investigation."

"No problem," the fire chief agreed and walked off.

Colby was joined shortly after by the police detective assigned to the case. "I've had officers questioning the building's tenants. We had several sightings of two lone male figures fleeing from the apartment. They ran past that building. Unfortunately, that path leads to the main road. If there was a car waiting, they could have hopped inside and been long gone before the police even arrived. We'll pull surveillance video to see if we can spot them."

Colby pulled out his business card and repeated his request to the detective just as he had the fire chief.

The detective took the card and nodded. "I suppose you'll be taking over this investigation?"

He heard the resentment in the detective's tone. One of his officers had been killed. He had the right to be angry.

"We're not taking over, but we would like to be kept in the loop. Contact Olivia Mitchell from my office. She can probably give you some leads on the man who murdered your officer."

He seemed pleased to hear that they were free to work the murder angle for now. He turned and pointed back to the ravaged building. "Glad we're not investigating two murders. That's thanks to you."

Colby thanked him and gave condolences for his fallen officer. He didn't want recognition. He should have ended this months ago when Tessa was first murdered. That her home had burned down only added insult to injury, and now an officer was dead. The killer shouldn't have been allowed to operate all these months.

This was all his fault.

Brooke looked much better by the time Colby made it to the hospital. They'd cleaned her up, and she was sitting on a gurney in the emergency room area.

Tears glistened in her eyes when she spotted him, and her chin quivered. He pulled her into a hug. She clung to him for longer than he thought she would.

"I don't like hospitals," she told him as he slid into a chair opposite her.

He'd taken time to run by his place and shower and change, making certain to have someone posted by her room for protection until he arrived. "The good news is it doesn't look like they're going to keep you here. You should be discharged soon."

That didn't seem to please her. Her face fell, and he was certain she was thinking about where she was going to go. "I guess I'll check into a hotel."

"I had another idea. I think we should return to Courtland. We can stay at my brother's cabin. We can do a better job of keeping you safe if we go there."

"They already know about Courtland. Why would I be any safer there than in Dallas?"

"They might know about Courtland, but they don't know about the Silver Star. Besides, at the ranch, my brothers can be there to help protect you. We can lock the place down."

"I don't like the idea of hiding."

"These people aren't amateurs, Brooke. We're talking about a terrorist organization that has its sights on you. It's obvious they've given up on trying to abduct you and having you lead them to the information Tessa collected. They tried to kill you this time, and they nearly succeeded." His voice cracked with emotion as he recalled seeing the apartment on fire and finding her barely conscious on the floor. His heart had nearly stopped at the sight.

"At least think about it. You need to rest and recuperate. We can link up with the FBI through video conferencing so we won't lose the ability to use their resources. Plus, my brothers include a sheriff, a former deputy, a navy SEAL and a US Marshal. Not to mention, Josh's roster of deputies that includes my brother-in-law and my father, who is a former sheriff. We can keep you safe there. It doesn't mean we're giving up. We're just..." He searched for the right word. "We're just regrouping. Will you at least think about it?"

She nodded.

She'd liked Courtland, so he hoped that was in his favor. Returning to the Silver Star had been Josh's idea, but it was a good one. She needed time to rest, and it wasn't like she had Tessa's apartment to go back to. Not anymore. They'd burned it down. And he'd received word they'd torched her office as well. Anything to make certain no one uncovered the evidence Tessa had collected.

"Okay." She reached for his hand and held it.

Lightning streaked up Colby's arm. He could be having a heart attack from the electricity that sparked between them, but he wouldn't have even known it. He was too captivated by her beautiful green eyes.

He had to maintain his cool if he was going to keep Brooke safe. He'd already let her down. Those attacks against her should never have happened. What would he do if the killer or killers got to her again?

He steeled himself against that happening. Not on his watch. He would keep her safe no matter what it took. He was grateful to have the support of his family. Returning to Courtland was the right move.

"I'll make the arrangements. Don't worry. We'll make certain we aren't followed when we leave town."

"I trust you," she told him, and her simple declaration sent his emotions spinning out of control. She trusted him. She had placed her trust in a man who'd already failed so many times, a man who'd played a role in getting her cousin killed.

He steeled himself against his own self-doubt. He wouldn't let her down. He couldn't, or she was dead.

Why had she told him she trusted him?

As he walked out of the room to make the arrangements for their return to Courtland, Brooke's own words troubled her. They'd slipped out in a moment of weakness, and the expression on his face when he'd heard them had nearly done her in. It meant something to him that she trusted him.

But the truth was she wasn't sure she did.

She wanted to trust him. Everything inside her wanted to, but she'd already been through so much and had been disappointed so many times.

He blamed himself for what was happening to her and for not protecting Tessa. While it wasn't his fault, she couldn't discount the idea that something in his guilt was justified. Had he done something to pressure Tessa into getting involved in this?

She didn't know. She still didn't have the answers she needed, so staying in Dallas seemed the best plan.

But when she recalled the beauty and serenity of the ranch, she wavered. She needed out of the line of fire, if only for a day or two to regain her strength.

Then, she was coming at these guys and getting the answers she needed, no matter the cost.

The SUV was silent except for the hum of the tires on the road. The drive to Courtland was awkward. She still wasn't certain this was the safest plan, yet they'd taken every precaution. Colby had made sure of it. For that, she was grateful.

She wasn't looking forward to hiding away at his family's ranch, but she recalled how quiet and peaceful it had been at his brother's cabin, and suddenly a little peace and solitude suited her.

He broke the silence. "You've met my brother Josh. I have three other brothers—Lawson, Paul and Miles—and a sister, Kellyanne. You'll also meet my sisters-in-law, Bree, Melissa and Shelby, and my brother-in-law, Zeke."

All those siblings had her head spinning. "I hope there's not a test. I'm not sure I can remember them all." Being an only child with Tessa as the closest thing to family had her in awe of this large family and their close-knit bond.

"Don't worry about it. We'll be staying at Josh's cabin, and my brothers will take shifts keeping watch. I don't believe there's much to worry about. Like I said, these guys might know about Courtland but they don't know about the Silver Star."

"You don't think they can find that out? Everyone at the hospital knew Tessa was dating an FBI agent. It wouldn't be difficult to find you." She turned to look at him. "I did."

"Yes, you did. How did you find me?"

"I still have some contacts in the intelligence community. I might have called in a favor or two."

"For the location of an FBI agent, you probably had to call in six or seven favors."

Her face warmed. "It was a good friend who knows me and was confident I wasn't going to do anything harmful to you." She'd taken a big risk making that call, but she'd found him. Together, they would solve this case.

Colby's phone rang in the holder on the dash. He tapped the screen and Josh's voice filled the SUV. "What's your ETA?"

"About a half hour. We're nearly to Courtland. I just turned off the Ashbury Highway and we're heading west on Jones—" He stopped talking, glanced in the rearview mirror and gripped the steering wheel tighter.

She looked back and saw a car in the distance. "What's the matter?"

He pulled his gun from the holster and placed it on his lap. "I think we're being followed."

"Are you sure?" Josh asked from the phone.

She looked into Colby's eyes and saw certainty there. Her heart kicked up a notch. "Speed up. Let's see what he does."

He did as she suggested. The car sped up too, holding its distance but keeping up with them.

Colby took a sharp right turn and moments later the car did the same. "We are definitely being followed." His face was grim as he glanced at her. "We've been made. I'm sorry. I thought we'd taken all the precautions."

"This isn't your fault, Colby. Just get us out of here."

"I'm heading that way and sending a team," Josh insisted. "Let's capture these guys and get some answers."

She felt better knowing that Josh and his deputies were on their way. Being this isolated out in the middle of nowhere had her worried. If they chose to attack now, she and Colby would be sitting ducks. She wished she had her gun, but it had been in the apartment when it burned.

She turned in her seat, keeping an eye on the car behind them. It sped up and closed the distance between them. She reached for Colby's shoulder to warn him. "They're making their move."

His body was tense, his muscles tight. "I see it."

Suddenly, another vehicle appeared and pulled around them. "There's another car!"

Colby floored it, but the car quickly sped up and

caught up with them. It rammed them, trying to shove the SUV off the road.

"Hang on," Colby shouted as he fought to keep them on the road.

Suddenly, the window on the other car lowered.

"Gun!" He swerved as a gun fired, blasting through their windshield and creating a cracked spray pattern. Colby jerked the wheel, but another shot, this time at the tires, sent them skidding off the road. The SUV flipped, rolling down the embankment. Each slam against the ground echoed with her screams. They landed hard upside down several feet from the road.

Brooke's head pounded, and her entire body ached from the impact, but she was alive and conscious. She looked over at Colby. He was out cold in his seat. Blood pooled from a gash on his head.

The screeching of tires caused her to look through the cracked window. The cars that had run them off the road were now parked up the hill, and several men got out. Brooke unlocked her seat belt and searched the car for the gun Colby had had in his lap. She found it. If she had to hold them off until Josh and his men arrived, she would do so. She didn't know if they were here to try to abduct her again or to kill them both, but she wasn't going to wait around to find out. They wouldn't take her without a fight.

She gripped the gun. It wasn't the first time she'd been pinned down and had to fight her way out of a situation, but at least this time she knew help was on the way.

Colby groaned and tried to sit up.

Treat Yourself with 2 Free Books!

GET UP TO 4 FREE BOOKS & 2 FREE GIFTS WORTH OVER $20

See Inside For Details

Claim Them While You Can

Get ready to relax and indulge with your **FREE BOOKS** and more!

Claim up to FOUR NEW BOOKS & TWO MYSTERY GIFTS – absolutely FREE!

Dear Reader,

We both know life can be difficult at times. That's why it's important to treat yourself so you can relax and recharge once in a while.

And I'd like to help you do this by sending you this amazing offer of up to FOUR brand new full length FREE BOOKS that WE pay for.

This is everything I have ready to send to you right now:

Try **Love Inspired® Romance Larger-Print** books and fall in love with inspirational romances that take you on an uplifting journey of faith, forgiveness and hope.

Try **Love Inspired® Suspense Larger-Print** books where courage and optimism unite in stories of faith and love in the face of danger.

Or **TRY BOTH!**

All we ask in return is that you answer 4 simple questions on the attached Treat Yourself survey. You'll get **Two Free Books** and **Two Mystery Gifts** from each series you try, *altogether worth over $20*! Who could pass up a deal like that?

Sincerely,

Pam Powers

Harlequin Reader Service

Treat Yourself to Free Books and Free Gifts.

Answer 4 fun questions and get rewarded.

▶ DETACH AND MAIL CARD TODAY!

	YES	NO
1. I LOVE reading a good book.	◯	◯
2. I indulge and "treat" myself often.	◯	◯
3. I love getting FREE things.	◯	◯
4. Reading is one of my favorite activities.	◯	◯

TREAT YOURSELF • Pick your 2 Free Books...

Yes! Please send me my Free Books from each series I select and Free Mystery Gifts. I understand that I am under no obligation to buy anything, as explained on the back of this card.

Which do you prefer?

❏ **Love Inspired® Romance Larger-Print** 122/322 IDL GRDP
❏ **Love Inspired® Suspense Larger-Print** 107/307 IDL GRDP
❏ **Try Both** 122/322 & 107/307 IDL GRED

FIRST NAME   LAST NAME

ADDRESS

APT.#   CITY

STATE/PROV.   ZIP/POSTAL CODE

EMAIL ❏ Please check this box if you would like to receive newsletters and promotional emails from Harlequin Enterprises ULC and its affiliates. You can unsubscribe anytime.

LI/SLI-520-TY22

"Be still," she whispered to him.

Suddenly, he jerked upright. "What's happening?"

"The car flipped. We're pinned down."

He grunted. "I can't move my leg."

She looked and saw that his foot was caught beneath the dash. "Is it broken?"

"I don't think so, just trapped. Josh is on his way. We just have to hold them off until then."

She glanced through the shattered pattern on the window at a group of four men gathered around the car. How long before they came after her and Colby? And what were they waiting for?

"Where's my phone?" Colby scrambled around and found it on the floorboard. The screen was shattered. "It won't work. Don't worry. Josh knows where we are. They'll find us."

She only hoped it was in time.

She did a scope of the area. No houses. No buildings in sight. And with Colby's leg pinned, even if they could free him, there was nowhere to run. They were trapped. It was either fight or surrender. She preferred to fight. These men were likely involved in her cousin's murder in some way. It was tempting to go with them just to get the answers she sought, but she wasn't that foolish. They would probably just kill her anyway.

But Colby wasn't in any position to defend himself. She needed to get him out of the line of fire. It was her they wanted. She checked that the gun was loaded and ready, and scanned the area for a safe place to take cover and draw their fire. A group of downed trees and rocks across the clearing would do the trick.

"I'm going to make a run for that cover over there. Hopefully, they'll follow me and leave you alone."

He gripped her arm. "I can't let you do that."

This wasn't the time for his overprotectiveness to rear its head. "We only have one gun, Colby. We have to make do until your brother arrives. If they find you trapped, they may just kill you on the spot."

His mind seemed to be playing out different scenarios, ones that didn't put her in danger. He wouldn't come up with one. This was their only play if they were to both remain alive.

She didn't want him to think she was abandoning him, so she leaned down and kissed his lips, surprised at herself for her action. She'd meant it as a quick peck, but the moment their lips touched, she knew she'd wanted to do this for a while. He responded to her, and she had to force herself to break away. They were in serious danger, and she didn't have time to lose herself in Colby's embrace.

She pulled back, slipped out the broken window and scurried across the field.

SEVEN

Her mind was still reeling. What had she been thinking kissing him? She crouched behind a rock formation and watched as the men approached the overturned SUV. They obviously hadn't seen her sneak out of it.

Brooke took a fortifying breath and fired off a few rounds, sending them scurrying for cover. Good. They needed to take cover. Thankfully, they were ignoring the SUV, as she'd hoped. She fired more shots and took cover when they returned fire. She checked her ammunition. She couldn't hold off four men with guns all on her own for long.

She heard the sound of sirens in the distance. The men scrambled to their cars and took off, sending dust flying as they drove away.

Brooke sighed with relief and then ran back to the SUV. Colby lay on the overturned hood, his foot still captured beneath the dash and his face red with anger and frustration.

"They're gone," she told him.

"That was a dumb thing to do, Brooke. What if they

had killed you or taken you? I wouldn't have been able to do anything."

"You were trapped. That was our best shot, Colby. I did what I had to do."

"It wasn't smart."

"You're still alive, aren't you?" Anger bristled through her. "I'm not some helpless female, and it's not my first time shooting a gun, remember? Don't think for a moment that I can't survive without you, Colby Avery." She stood to run up the hill to flag down his brother, but she couldn't resist poking her head back inside the SUV for one last barb. "Oh, and you're welcome for saving your life."

She hustled away and waved her arms. Several vehicles slammed to a stop in front of her while others hurried after the cars that had sped away.

Josh hopped from his truck and ran toward Brooke, his gaze focusing on the overturned SUV. "Where's Colby? Is he okay?"

"He's fine. His foot is trapped from when we rolled, but he's otherwise okay."

Relief flooded his expression. He pulled out his radio and called for an ambulance and the fire department. "We may have to cut him out." He walked to the vehicle, leaned down and peeked inside. "How you doing, man?"

"Physically okay. My pride has taken a hit though. Did you catch up with those guys?"

"My men are following, trying to pick up their trail. We'll find them. You hold tight. Help is on the way." He pulled Brooke aside. "What happened?"

"They ambushed us and ran us off the road. I held them off until they heard the sirens."

"How did they even know you were coming here?"

That was the big question. They must have been watching her more closely than they'd suspected. She glanced around at all the police activity but still didn't feel safe. The feeling of constantly being watched wasn't far from her mind. This group had their sights zeroed in on her, and they were determined to see her dead, just like her cousin.

She covered her arms with her hands to try to wipe away the goose bumps that rose on her arms. She was ready to be inside, out of sight. But would she ever feel safe again?

Colby felt the fire department took their sweet time cutting him loose. Finally, his foot was free, and he was able to crawl out of the overturned vehicle.

His ankle ached, and he allowed the paramedics to check him out. They agreed with him that it wasn't broken, but it wasn't only his foot that was aching. His ego had taken another blow too. He didn't like knowing that Brooke had had to take matters into her own hands to protect herself and him. He was the one who was supposed to be doing the protecting, but he'd done a terrible job so far. How was he even contributing to her safety at all?

One of the paramedics, a guy he knew from high school, shone a light in his eye. "You need to go to the hospital. You lost consciousness during the wreck. You should get checked out."

"I'm fine. I'm not going to the hospital," he insisted. He was much more concerned with getting Brooke to the ranch and to the safety of its borders than sitting through a bunch of tests that would tell what he already knew. He was fine except for some aches and pains and a swollen ankle.

Josh gave him a look that said he needed to take care of himself, but Colby knew his brother wouldn't make that demand on him. "Well, if you're not going to the hospital, let's get you both to the house."

He nodded. That was exactly what he wanted. "Any word on the men who ran us off the road?" Colby asked him.

He shook his head and had a grim look on his face. "No. They found the vehicles abandoned on the side of the road. They must have had someone pick them up or had another vehicle stashed somewhere. I've got my team working on stolen-vehicle reports, but so far, no one has reported anything."

Colby stood and tried to limp toward his brother's truck. Brooke came up beside him and put his arm over her shoulders. "Let me help you," she told him.

The feel of her against him sent his mind thinking about that kiss. About the lingering, savory delight of every moment. His lips were still buzzing at the sensation. But it had been more than that. It had been a resounding declaration that she trusted him even if he didn't deserve it.

He did his best not to lean on her too much, but he had to admit she was a help. He needed to be back on his feet fast. He was no good to her with a bum foot.

He was supposed to be protecting her, not the other way around.

She slid into the back seat of Josh's truck while he crawled into the front. Josh slipped behind the steering wheel and took off. Colby couldn't help glancing again at the SUV. The damage was massive. They were fortunate to have gotten off with such minor injuries. Those men must not have been firing to kill them. They'd shot at the windows and the tires, more proof that they'd meant to stop them and probably abduct Brooke. Were these guys back to that again? Or maybe they just wanted to see what they could get out of her before they killed them both?

Either way, it was something else that he and Brooke had survived no thanks to him, and that stung. She'd taken control when she'd needed to. He should be thankful, but it rubbed him the wrong way. He didn't know why. It wasn't because she was a woman. He'd worked with female agents who were just as competent as he was. And Brooke had training. But still, it stung, and Colby was sure it had more to do with Tessa and his failure to keep her alive. Was he trying to make up for that by keeping Brooke safe? If he was, it wasn't working.

Tessa had been killed because he hadn't taken her claims seriously enough to offer her the protection she'd deserved. He couldn't deny he'd been glad to hear from her, but when he'd realized she'd called him that day to tell him about her suspicions, his pride had been hurt. He'd been hoping for a reconciliation, but she'd only wanted him for his FBI credentials.

He breathed a sigh of relief when Josh turned the

truck off the main road and under the Silver Star signage. It felt good to be home. This was his safe place, his comfort, the one place he didn't feel like he had to explain himself to anyone.

Josh parked in front of the main house. The front door opened, and he spotted his mom and dad step onto the porch, followed by several members of his family. He'd told Brooke all about them. He was glad they were all there, but he wasn't relishing their knowing that he'd dropped the ball again on keeping another woman safe.

He got out, and his mother hurried out to him. Her face was full of horror and worry as she looked over the cuts and bruises and saw how he was limping. "Colby! Are you okay? Josh told us what happened."

He shot his brother a glare for worrying her and then gave his mom a hug. "I'm fine. Just a little beaten up. When you see the SUV, you'll know we escaped something."

He turned to Brooke, who was climbing out of the back seat. She, too, had her own scrapes and bruises, and she was covered in dirt. Her hair was messy, yet she still managed to look beautiful. "Mom, Dad, everyone, this is Brooke Moore."

"Nice to meet you," Brooke said, reaching out to shake his mom's hand.

His mother looked confused and then looked to Colby. "You too... Brooke?" She glanced at Colby. "I don't understand. You said Tessa..."

He'd forgotten the resemblance for a moment. His mother had never met Tessa, but she'd seen pictures of her and must think Colby was pulling some kind of switcheroo on her. "Brooke is Tessa's cousin. Their mothers were identical twins and, yes, there's a very strong resemblance between them, but I promise you, this is Brooke, not Tessa."

"Oh, well, that explains it. Welcome, Brooke."

"Thank you, Mrs. Avery. It's nice to meet you."

He introduced her to the entire group. Only his brother Miles and his wife, Melissa, were missing. They were expected to arrive at the ranch in a few hours for Miles to help with protection detail. That was just like his family. They banded together when it was necessary, and he was thankful for their willingness to do so. He glanced at his sister and felt his face warm at the memory of yet another failure of his. He was especially grateful she was safe after he'd nearly gotten her and her son killed.

He had to get it together. Brooke's life depended on it.

Paul approached him. "Lawson, Zeke and I are going to take shifts patrolling the area around the cabin."

"Count me in on that rotation."

"Okay, but you need to get some rest first."

He tried to shake away his brother's concern. "I'm fine."

"No, you're not. You're injured and worn out. Get some rest and let us handle this for now. Maybe in a day or so, you can relieve us."

He didn't like being sidelined, despite having excluded himself from this case weeks ago. He finally agreed to let them take over for a while. Isn't that why he'd talked Brooke into coming here? To get his brothers' help? It made no sense for him to refuse it now.

They climbed back into the truck, and Josh drove them to the cabin.

Colby limped up the front porch steps and fell onto the couch in the living room. Josh chucked his brother's belongings in the spare bedroom, where he'd stayed before. He then pointed Brooke toward his bedroom and deposited her bag inside. "The bedding has been changed, and I've moved some of my personal stuff out. It's all yours for as long as you need it."

"Thank you, Josh." She gave Colby a weary glance before disappearing through the door.

Colby knew Josh hadn't had much stuff in there anyway, but he, too, appreciated the gesture.

"So what's the plan?" he asked his brother.

"The plan is for you and Brooke to remain here and recuperate for a day or two. I'll retrieve any belongings you and Brooke brought. I can also help you set up the computer info if you need it."

"Thanks, but I think I can handle that." Much of his equipment was still here from his previous stay with his brother, so connecting to the FBI offices wouldn't be much of a hardship. He would be glad to get his hands on the files that had been in the back of his now totaled SUV. No one had thought to grab them in the aftermath of the wreck. He hoped they were still intact.

Josh glanced at the bedroom door. "How is it going with Brooke?"

"Not great. I can't figure out how to help her. It

seems wherever we go, whatever we do, this group is on top of us."

"Is it possible they're listening to you or have someone inside the FBI?"

"A mole in the agency? I doubt that. A listening device might be an interesting thing to check out though." He reached for his phone to call Olivia to have her check his and Brooke's phones for unusual tracking or cloning apps. Then he remembered his phone had been damaged in the wreck. "Well, I guess if they were listening, they're not any longer."

"I'll send someone to the store to get you another phone, and one for Brooke too."

"I also need my gun. Did you get it back from Brooke?"

"I did." He retrieved it from the truck and handed it to Colby. "I'll also have Paul bring you another gun and some more ammunition. I doubt you'll need it out here, but better safe than sorry."

"Thanks, Josh."

"No problem. Mom's going to have some food sent over. She and Dad will make sure you're both fed until you've recovered. Until then, I would remain inside as much as possible and take it easy. Doctor's orders."

"What doctor? I didn't go to the hospital."

"And thanks for not telling Mom that. She'll be hustling over here to give you the once-over herself when she finds out you lost consciousness."

"It wasn't for long. I'm fine."

Josh nodded. "If I thought you weren't, I wouldn't have brought you home. I would have taken you straight to the ER." He headed for the door. "I'll call if we find out anything else."

"Better use the computer to video chat until I get my phone replaced," Colby reminded him.

"Yeah, I'll remember that. Get some rest."

His brother walked out, and Colby slid down into the cushions of the couch. His head was pounding right along with the pulse in his swollen ankle. He placed his foot on the coffee table to elevate it. His ankle was swollen and painful, and he wanted some Tylenol or something for the pain, but it hurt too much to get up to find it. Instead, he settled back on the couch and closed his eyes.

He was in a safe place where he could finally relax for a few hours and let his brothers handle security. It felt good to let go of the worry and fear that had plagued him since the day he'd met Brooke. He didn't blame her for that. He'd been a mess before she'd showed up due to his failure to protect Tessa, but Brooke's arrival and her being suddenly thrust into danger had sent his wheels spinning again.

He felt something on his foot and jerked up, surprised to find that he'd fallen asleep. Brooke jumped back. He saw she'd placed an ice pack on his ankle.

"I thought it might help with the swelling," she told him. "I didn't mean to wake you."

"No, that's great. Thanks." He rubbed his eyes. "How long have I been out?"

"Three hours."

He hadn't meant to sleep, but his head felt better. His body was still aching, and his ankle was on fire, but the cooling relief of the ice pack was already helping. "I didn't mean to fall asleep."

"You needed it. I took a short nap myself."

"How are you feeling?"

"I'm sore from the wreck, but I'm okay. I'm glad we're here. Despite this setback, I think you were right. Coming was a good idea. I feel better knowing your brothers are keeping watch."

"You're safe here. I promise." He'd said those words before and things had gone badly. This time, he prayed that wouldn't be the case.

She gave his hand a squeeze, stood and walked to the kitchen area. "I found some canned goods in the cupboard and was about to heat up a can of soup. Would you like some?"

His stomach growled in response to her query. "I could eat."

She grinned, obviously having heard his stomach grumbling. "Soup coming up." She opened a can of soup and heated it on the stove before pouring them both a mug and handing one to him. She also dug out some crackers from the cupboard and then sank into the chair across from him.

The hot liquid was just what he needed. "It's good. Thank you."

She smiled and munched on a cracker. He could see she was moving slowly, but at least she could move. She'd been through a lot over the past few days.

"I can hardly mess up soup, can I?"

"What does that mean? You don't cook?"

She shook her head. "Not really. I always wanted to

learn, but I never really had anyone to teach me, and I never took the time to learn on my own once I was grown. Besides, my life hasn't really been conducive to home-cooked meals."

"Surely there were downtimes." She hadn't talked much about her work for the army, and he hadn't pried, mostly because he'd assumed much of it was classified. He didn't talk about his work to strangers much either, so he'd assumed it was something similar, and talking about her time in the army seemed to make her sad.

"I joined the army right out of high school. I traveled a lot with my job. There wasn't much downtime. My job became my life. When I started dating Jack… well, our relationship and our work sort of merged."

"Jack?"

She nodded. "My supervisor. We met when he recruited me for his team. We spent nearly all our time together."

He didn't care for the twinge of jealousy that surfaced in his gut. "I haven't seen you call him." And why kiss him if she had a boyfriend?

"We broke up months ago. When I left the army behind, I left him behind too."

"I'm sorry." He didn't want to pry into her private life, but he desperately wanted to know what had happened. He took a sip of his soup. If she wanted him to know, she would tell him, but it broke his heart to see the pain in her expression, pain he didn't think came from her injuries.

"What about you and Tessa? You said she broke up

with you before she died? Was it really just about your job?"

He set down his cup of soup and, when he looked back at her, he swore he saw suspicion in her face. "It wasn't anything bad. I mean, nothing happened. I was working an assignment tracking down a suspected serial killer. I wasn't even the lead on the assignment. I was only there for backup. But we cornered the suspect in an old factory warehouse. We ended up in a gunfight, and I got hit in the shoulder. It wasn't a bad wound. I've had a lot worse, but when Tessa saw it, everything seemed to change. I guess she was confronted with the reality that my job can be dangerous. She couldn't handle it."

"Really? She ended your relationship over that?"

He nodded. He hadn't wanted it to end, but he'd respected her decision. He'd prayed she would change her mind, but he'd also known it took a special person to be the spouse of a law enforcement officer.

"I saw the picture of you two on her desk. She still had it there."

He felt his face warm. She hadn't given up on him completely. He wasn't sure if he was glad to hear that or sad that he hadn't pressed her. "We'd only dated a few months before my shooting, but I cared a lot for her. I think it could have gotten serious if she'd given us a chance, but I also know not everyone can handle being married to someone with a dangerous profession."

"I guess I can understand that. It wasn't an issue with me and Jack since we were both in the same profession. It never occurred to me."

"Did you never date anyone who wasn't in the army?"

She shook her head. "No. All of my previous relationships were somehow connected to the army. None of them was serious, except for Jack. At least, I thought we were serious." She set down her soup and leaned back in her chair. "Until he cheated on me."

The pain in those words stabbed him. It explained her guarded behavior. "I'm sorry. That's terrible."

"Him not telling me about Tessa's death was worse. He said he didn't want to jeopardize the operation by pulling me out."

Anger bit through him. Her ex had had no right to do such a thing.

"Any lingering feelings I had for him ended once I discovered what he'd done. By that time, it was too late to return home. I'd missed the funeral. So I applied for bereavement leave. My enlistment is up in a few months, and I have enough saved up vacation days to make it until then."

"So you're not going back to the army? What will you do?"

"Honestly, I have no idea. The only thing I've been able to think about for the past four months is figuring out who killed my cousin. I have no idea what life after that will look like."

"No plans at all? You've never thought about what you might do after your army career?"

"Honestly, I never thought about leaving the army. I loved what I did. I enjoyed the investigative part, and working undercover didn't bother me either. I guess I liked the idea of stepping into a make-believe life even if it was for a short time. Until Tessa was killed, I never thought about what the future held. Since she died though, whenever I try to think about the future, it's empty." She seemed to lose herself for a moment before shaking it off. "What about you? Did you always want to be an FBI agent?"

"Absolutely. I had the FBI in my sights when I was in college. My dad was the local sheriff, and law enforcement has always been in my blood. In fact, aside from Josh, my brother Lawson was a deputy for a while until he decided to take over the running of the ranch. My brother Miles is a US Marshal, and of course, Josh followed our dad and grandfather into the sheriff's office. There was never any doubt that I would go into law enforcement in some capacity."

"And you like what you're doing?"

He nodded. "I do. I enjoy my work. I like getting bad guys off the street. I detest people who prey on others. In my opinion, they're the scum of the earth."

"I can't disagree with you. A lot of my job was searching out people who posed a threat to our country. You can't imagine the people looking to sell out the nation for a few bucks."

He'd seen it firsthand. Even now, this radical group that had targeted Brooke was said to have anti-government ideologies. "I can certainly understand how people can get disillusioned with the government, but putting innocent lives at risk is where I draw the line with my sympathies."

"Agreed." She stood, moving slowly as she gathered their cups and returned to the kitchen to place them into the sink. "I'm going to call it a night and try to get some more rest. You should do the same. Want me to help you to the bedroom?"

He shook his head. "I'm going to sit here for a while. I can make it to the bedroom, but for right now, me and this couch are glued at the hip."

"Okay, good night, Colby."

"Good night, Brooke."

She walked back into the bedroom and closed the door.

He leaned back into the cushions. The pain in her life broke his heart. He sometimes forgot how well he had it until he met someone who was worse off than him. At least he had his family to back him up when he needed it. Brooke had no one.

No one but him.

He couldn't let her down again.

Before he fell asleep, he sent up a silent prayer that God would lead them to answers about who was after Brooke and why, and help him and Brooke stop them.

The morning sun poured in through the curtains, dragging Brooke from a finally restful sleep. She got up and got dressed, and was surprised when she didn't see Colby when she left her room. Glancing at the clock, she realized she'd slept for sixteen hours and it was already late morning. She'd needed it and did feel better.

She heard footsteps and talking outside. Panic gripped her for a moment. She wished for her gun. She was going to have to get another one somehow.

She walked to the window and spotted one of Colby's

brothers, Lawson she thought, sitting atop a saddled horse and holding the reins to another.

She opened the front door and stepped outside onto the porch. "What's going on?" she asked Colby.

Colby turned to her and smiled. "I thought we might take a ride."

He'd showered and shaved and looked absolutely gorgeous in his jeans and boots. The swelling in his ankle must have gone down for him to put those on. The smell of his leathery aftershave caught on the breeze and tickled her nose. "Is that safe?"

"We won't go far. I just thought it might be nice to get outside for a while. Maybe work out the kinks in my muscles. What do you say?"

"She's real gentle," Lawson assured her about the horse.

"Besides, I'll be right here with you." Colby hefted his foot up into the stirrup, a slight grimace the only indication that his ankle was bothering him. He mounted the horse and took the reins then reached his hand out to her. "What do you say? Take a ride with me?"

She wasn't an experienced rider and would never have been comfortable on her own horse. Knowing he was going to do the steering made a difference. A ride with her arms wrapped around Colby? How could she say no to that?

Lawson got off his horse and walked over to her, obviously intent on helping her up. Still, she hesitated. "I-I'm not sure."

"It's okay," Lawson assured her. "Colby won't let anything happen to you."

It was a promise Colby'd made her several times over. So far, despite multiple attempts on her life, he'd kept it. She was safe with him. That certainty gave her the courage to accept his hand and mount the horse with Lawson's help.

"Now put your arms around my waist," Colby instructed.

Her face warmed at the idea of holding on to him. She was glad he couldn't see it and turned her head away so, hopefully, Lawson couldn't either. She had to stop having such feelings about this man. Despite her attraction to him, she couldn't let her heart go down that road only to get broken again.

"You ready?" Colby asked, giving her a side glance.

She nodded and tightened her grip around his middle. "I think so." Her heart was hammering nervously as he nudged the horse into a walk, but she was more centered on the feeling of his muscles as they moved and on the hand he'd gently placed over hers.

"We'll take it nice and slow at first."

She didn't care for the "at first" part, but she slowly relaxed, undug her nose from his back and took in the scenery unfolding before her. The Silver Star was beautiful this time of year. The green grass and blooming flowers set against a clear blue sky. It looked to her like something out of a fairy tale. She'd never seen the countryside, at least not like this. She was used to the city streets and the battle-torn parts of the world. When had she ever seen anything so clean and untouched?

It took her breath away. "It's beautiful here."

Colby chuckled. "It is. I sometimes forget. Being

in the city, you get used to the noise and the concrete, but everything out here is just like it was a hundred years ago."

He pulled the horse to a stop in front of a pond, slid off and helped her down, his strong arms holding her as he lowered her to the ground. She sucked in a breath, remembering the feel of his lips against hers when she'd kissed him.

He released her and took her hand to lead her toward the water. They sat together on the ground, and he played with a strand of grass and stared out at the landscape.

"Being in the city, it's so easy to get lost in the hustle and go-go-go of that lifestyle. Sometimes, I forget to stop and be thankful for everything I have. But life slows down here. Here, I have time to admire and appreciate everything God has given us."

She couldn't help the way her hand stiffened when he spoke of God. She pulled away and fiddled with a strand of grass. "What has God given me? Nothing." She hadn't meant to say that aloud, but he'd heard it.

"That's not true. It can't be true." He leaned back and watched her, his blue eyes probing for answers to questions he didn't dare ask.

She hated the emptiness that filled her when he spoke of God. "Tessa was the one with the faith. Somehow, she saw everything with optimism. She always said everything would work out because God was in control. Only, God hasn't been very active in my life. I was orphaned when I was a child. My aunt Melinda raised me and Tessa the best she could, but she was always gone, always working. We spent most of our days alone. Tessa had friends. She always had friends, but I spent most of my time at home by myself, usually with my head stuck in a book, dreaming of adventure and new places."

He grinned at her. "A dreamer. I knew it."

She laughed at his good-natured teasing tone. "I guess that's why I joined the army right out of high school. I was seeking that adventure."

"Did you find it?"

"I guess I did. I loved my job, the structure of army life, the travel."

"Then why leave it?"

She thought about Jack and her unit. His affair hadn't been the only thing that had influenced her decision. "Just disillusioned, I guess. Sometimes, all you can see is the bad stuff of the world."

He sat up. "God didn't make the mess and the chaos, Brooke." He stretched out his hand to the picturesque landscape. "He made the beauty. He made the goodness. Man and sin corrupted it all."

She didn't see much beauty in herself. She had gotten to a place once where she'd felt comfortable in her own skin, but Jack's betrayal had sent her spinning with self-doubt. She stared at Colby and sighed. "I haven't seen much beauty in my life. It's mostly been war and bitterness. The few good things I've had have all ended in heartbreak. What kind of a god makes that?"

"God doesn't. He can't promise a peaceful life without trials, but He's always there with us. Hebrews 13:5 reveals God's promise that He will never leave us nor forsake us. And in Jeremiah 29:11, He promises hope and a future."

She shook her head. "Not for me."

Colby took her hand again and squeezed it. "Even when it seems you have no one in your life who cares about you, Brooke, you've still got Jesus. He's the only shoulder you need to lean on."

She wished she could believe as easily as he did, but she hadn't had that experience with God. "Tessa was the one with the faith. Her friends used to take her to church."

"You didn't go?"

She hated saying bad things about her cousin. "I loved Tessa like a sister, but she and I were very different people. She was extroverted and always on the go. I preferred staying home. She had her friends and I had mine. Only mine were usually books."

"I'm sorry. That must have been a lonely way to grow up. I always thought you and Tessa were close. I mean, she spoke like you and she were close."

"We were all each other had."

He put his hand on her back and left it there, and she didn't want him to move it. It was a supportive gesture and it meant the world to her. He heard her. He listened to her and didn't make fun of her.

"I loved my cousin, and I'll do whatever it takes to bring her killer to justice, but the truth is that our relationship had drifted from close to nearly nonexistent over the past decade."

"I'm sorry. It sounds like you've been on your own for a long, long time."

She nodded. "Yes. A very long time. Honestly, it never bothered me when I was focused on my work. Only, lately, after I learned about Jack's betrayal, I realized I want something more."

"You wanted to settle down? Start a family?"

She smiled. "I've thought of it. Like every bookworm, I love a good romance and always dreamed of having one myself. When I met Jack, I thought I had found that. I fell hard for him. But I suppose it just wasn't meant to be."

"I don't believe in meant-to-be," he told her. "Relationships take work. They're a responsibility that can't be ignored. Meant-to-be is a trite way of saying things should be easy. They're not always. My parents have been married for over forty years. I've watched them work at it. I try to give my relationships priority, but my job sometimes interferes with that."

"Like it did with Tessa?"

"Neither of us had easy jobs. Hers was sometimes just as demanding as mine."

"But still, her bad day at work didn't end up with her dying either, did it?"

He grinned and shrugged. "I guess not."

"I like your family."

"Thank you. I confess, I can't imagine what it's like not having a brother or sister you can pick up the phone and call whenever you need something. I've probably taken that for granted once too often in my lifetime. After Tessa died, Josh saw how devastated I was. If I hadn't had a place I could go that I knew people cared about me, I'm not sure what I would have done."

She pushed a strand of hair behind her ear. "Yeah, well, who needs backup when you have weaponry?" She tried to make light of it, but she was envious of what he had. He could pick up the phone at any time and have a sibling who had his back. She had no one to call. She was utterly alone.

Speaking of which… "I lost my gun in the apartment fire. I need another one. Can you arrange that?"

He nodded. "Are you sure that's a good idea?"

"I need something to protect myself, don't I?"

He seemed saddened by her comment, and she realized he considered himself her protector. She hadn't meant to diminish that. "I only meant that it's better if I can protect myself if I need to."

"I get it. I can arrange that."

He stood and dusted off his pants. "We should probably get back."

His good-natured manner had faded. He held out his hand to help her up. But if he was going to have his feelings hurt over her wanting a gun, she needed it more than ever.

He climbed onto the horse and pulled her up behind him, but things had changed. She could feel it.

She'd ruined something good between them.

More proof that she was utterly alone.

Colby dropped her off at the cabin, but he didn't dismount. "I'm going to meet my brothers over by the barn and get an update on security measures. My dad went into town this morning and got us each a new cell phone. You'll find yours charging in the kitchen. My number has been programmed into it, if you need to reach me. I won't be long."

He turned the horse and loped away.

Brooke fell onto a chair on the porch. This back-and-forth with Colby was getting old. She understood his desire to keep her protected, but she was perfectly capable of taking care of herself.

Might as well get her mind back on the case. Once they'd solved it and brought the killer or killers to justice, the question of whether or not she could take care of herself wouldn't matter.

She walked inside, pulled Colby's evidence board from the bedroom and propped it up on the kitchen countertop. Based on what she'd seen in his files, this board was thorough. Josh still hadn't brought them the files, but Brooke knew Olivia had emailed some of the information. It was now just a matter of finding a lead and following it to its logical conclusion.

She spent hours picking through lines of evidence, and like Colby, she came up empty. She decided to take a break just as a vehicle stopped in front of the cabin. Brooke peeked through the curtain to see an SUV with Courtland County Sheriff's Office decals parked. A woman got out and headed up the porch steps. Brooke met her at the door.

The pretty blonde gave her a wide smile. She wore a deputy's uniform and a sidearm on her hip. "I'm Cecile Richardson. We met when you first came to town."

Brooke remembered her. She'd helped with the investigations into both her near abductions. "What can I do for you, Deputy Richardson?"

"Please, it's Cecile. And I think I can do something for you." She walked back to her vehicle and returned with a hard case. She placed it on the patio table and popped the clips to reveal a handgun. She turned to Brooke and smiled. "Colby said you needed a new weapon."

Brooke sucked in a relieved breath. "Yes, I do. Mine was lost in a fire."

"Well, I can't in good conscience give you a gun without making certain you know how to use it." She shut the case, causing Brooke's hackles to rise. Why bring the gun here if she wasn't going to let her have it?

"I was trained in the army. I know how to use a weapon."

"Let's just make sure. Then we'll have to complete some paperwork to make certain you have the proper permit."

"I already have a permit to carry."

"Good. That makes things much simpler. Guns don't have to be registered in Texas. This one belongs to Josh, but he gave me permission to let you have it if I feel you can handle it." She walked down the porch steps to her SUV and turned to wait on Brooke.

If she wanted a weapon, and she did, she needed to do this. She retrieved the phone Colby had told her about and texted him, letting him know where she was and who she was with, then she climbed into the passenger's seat. Cecile got in too, drove down a dirt road through the pasture and stopped in front of a fence. A shed with a lock on it sat nearby.

"What's this place?"

"It's where Colby's brother Paul keeps his weapons and equipment for his tactical training seminars. He's also set up a small place for target practice."

She grabbed the case and handed it to Brooke. "Let's see how you do."

Cecile got out and walked toward the fence. In a bin were tin cans and bottles. She set them up in a line on the fence. It wasn't exactly a shooting range, but it would work. If Cecile wanted to make certain she knew how to handle a gun, Brooke had no problem showing her.

Cecile gave her a pair of safety glasses and moved out of the way. Brooke opened the case and checked the gun. It looked to be in good working condition but she checked it again once she had it loaded. Satisfied, she stood, took aim and fired several shots. Each hit its mark. It felt good to have a weapon back in her hands.

She took off her safety glasses and turned to Cecile, who smiled and nodded. "Nice job. I guess you do know how to handle yourself, don't you?"

"I told you. Eleven years in the army. I'm trained in all sorts of weaponry."

Cecile smiled again. "Girl after my own heart." She hurried over and reset another stack of cans and bottles on the fence line. She pushed Brooke aside, pulled her own gun and fired, hitting all the cans. She smiled when the last one hit the ground.

Brooke felt an instant connection to this woman and knew they could be friends. "You're a good shot."

"I grew up doing target practice with my brothers. Stomped them every time."

Hoofbeats thundered. They both turned and spotted Colby and Josh on horses heading their way.

Colby dropped from his mount. "We heard gunfire."

Brooke saw the confusion in his face sliding toward annoyance. "Just a little target practice."

Cecile motioned toward her. "She can handle herself, Colby."

"Shooting cans from a fence isn't a real test of accuracy." He didn't seem convinced, which fired up Brooke even more.

"Well, it's the best I can do right now. Would you prefer I took her off the ranch to the gun range?"

"I would prefer you talk with me first."

That comment shocked her. She'd thought Cecile was here at Colby's request. She turned to look at Cecile, who glared at Josh.

He shrugged as Colby turned to him. "You told me she wanted a gun. I took that to mean you wanted me to get her one."

"You thought wrong."

That was enough for her. Who was he to make that decision for her? "Listen here, Colby Avery. You don't get to decide what I can and can't do. You're not my boss or my boyfriend. I'm used to being able to protect myself, so if I want to get a gun, I will get one."

She pushed past him and started walking back to the cabin, her anger and annoyance growing with each step. How dare he think he could control what she did and who she talked to. He was just like Jack, thinking he knew what was best and trying to take her decisions out of her hands.

Horse hooves sounded behind her.

"Brooke, wait. Stop. Please stop." The horse trotted next to her. "I'm sorry. You're right. I wasn't trying to control you. I promise I wasn't. I was concerned."

"Well, I don't need your concern."

He stopped and slid off the horse. "You can't stop me from worrying about you."

She stopped and turned to him. "What do you want from me, Colby? I'm not your prisoner, and I'm not some damsel in distress that you need to rescue. I can take care of myself."

He nodded, his head down. "I know. You've proven that again and again. It's just… It's just—"

Anger burned through her. She knew the reason. "Every time you look at me, you see Tessa. Well, I'm not her. She might have needed your protection, but I don't." She started to walk off again, but his next words stopped her.

"You're right. She did need my protection, and I didn't give it to her." The angst in his voice was enough to make her turn back to him. Shame and guilt filled his face. "She reached out to me. She needed me, and I wasn't there for her."

"You didn't know she was in trouble. You didn't know they would kill her."

"I should have. Greed makes people do crazy things. I see it all the time."

"Tessa's death wasn't your fault, Colby. No one could have known that would happen to her."

"I knew. She called me. She said they were on to her and she was afraid. I was working on another case, and

I didn't give her concerns as much attention as I should have. I should have stopped what I was doing right then and taken her suspicions seriously."

She understood his regret and didn't blame him for Tessa's death, although she could see he blamed himself.

"You didn't kill her. Those men did, and they're the ones who have to answer for it. Them and the person who hired them."

"I know you're right. I just can't stop thinking that if I had stopped what I was doing—"

"Second-guessing yourself doesn't do anybody any good. We can't change the past. All we can do is move forward."

His blue eyes delved into hers. "Are you sure that's what you want to do, Brooke? Move forward with me?"

Her eyes widened and she took in a deep breath. She did want to move forward with him but not in the way he was asking. Or was he? What did he mean by that? His question sounded more personal than professional, and she felt her face warm at the idea of pursuing a relationship with this man.

He closed the distance between them and pushed a strand of hair behind her ear. The touch of his hand sent shivers pulsing through her. Her breath caught and she stared up into his deep-blue eyes. Losing herself in them would be so easy, giving her everything to him, falling into his embrace and never looking back.

His lips enveloped hers. The air around them seemed to electrify. She wrapped her arms around his neck and leaned into him. Yes. Her answer was yes. She wanted to move forward with him, but she'd already been burned once. Jack had proclaimed his love for her and then betrayed her and strung her along for the sake of the mission. Did Colby really want her? Or was he just using her to lure the killers out into the open?

Everything led back to his feelings for her cousin.

She pulled away from him even as her heart begged for more.

"What's wrong?"

"Nothing. I'm fine." She didn't want to look at him or he might see the fear in her heart, fear that his feelings for her weren't really for her. And she wasn't sure she could take it if she learned that was true.

He gave her some space, and she was glad. She needed it to pull herself back together.

"Let's head back to the cabin then."

Yes, back to the cabin where she could lock herself in the bedroom and cry herself to sleep.

He mounted the horse and reached out his hand to pull her up. She climbed up behind him and wrapped her arms around his waist, feeling hard muscle as he urged the horse into a walk.

She rested her head against his back. On any other day, this could be seen as a nice horseback ride through the ranch, but this wasn't just an ordinary spring day. Not after the kiss they'd just shared, and not when they had a group of extremists after them. Her biggest concern, however, was not letting Colby see how frightened she was at the thought of risking her heart.

A shot rang out, and the horse bucked, sending Brooke tumbling to the ground. She landed hard on her wrist, the pain pulsing through her. The horse neighed and bucked again as another shot rang out.

This time, Colby grabbed his chest before releasing the reins and falling to the ground as their mount bolted away.

EIGHT

Brooke reached for her gun and scanned the landscape. The only place the shooters could be was behind a patch of trees and bushes. She took aim and fired back, but that only resulted in more shots. She ran to Colby, grabbed his shirt and dragged him to cover. "How bad is it?"

He groaned but tried to play it off. "Not bad. It went all the way through."

She glanced at the back of his shoulder and saw he was right. The bullet had passed through. It looked to have missed the bones, which was good.

She stared out at the thicket of trees again. Using her ammunition at this range would do no good. They needed to get out of here.

Colby reached into his pocket and pulled out his cell phone. He went to dial his brother's number but didn't need to, because moments later, Cecile's SUV came roaring over the hill. She skidded to a stop in front of them. Josh hopped out with a gun and started firing at the tree line while Cecile and Brooke helped Colby into the back seat.

Once they were safely inside, Josh hopped back in and they took off.

"Are you both okay?" Cecile asked them.

"Colby was shot in the shoulder, but I don't think it's serious. It's a through and through."

"I was just about to call you," he told his brother.

"You didn't have to. We heard the gunfire. I called Paul and Lawson. They're setting up a perimeter. Maybe we can capture whoever was shooting at you."

Brooke hoped they did. She was ready for some answers as to why and who had paid for someone to kill her. Why was she still a target after all this time? They couldn't really still believe that she knew where the information Tessa collected was, could they? Especially not after they'd burned down her apartment and set fire to her office.

Cecile drove off the ranch and straight to the hospital. Colby didn't protest.

Brooke helped Colby out of the SUV and then waited with Josh and Cecile while he was seen by a doctor and bandaged up.

While they waited, Josh received a call from his brothers. The look on his face told her it wasn't good news even before he voiced it. "They got away."

She was disappointed but not shocked. The ranch was large enough for there to be plenty of places to hide and sneak around. She wasn't surprised that Paul and Lawson hadn't been able to find the men who'd shot at them.

"When is this going to end?" She hated the whiney tone of her voice, but she was so tired of this game and ready for it to be over. She wanted these men stopped. She wanted John Dutton, or whoever was behind it, put in jail.

Colby emerged from the emergency area with his arm in a sling and looking a little unstable. He insisted on going home despite the doctors wanting to keep him overnight.

"Watch out for infection," the nurse warned as they left.

Cecile took them back to the cabin, and Brooke helped him inside to the couch. He'd taken quite a beating since this all began, and she was worried about him. He needed a chance to rest and catch his breath. That was what they were both supposed to be doing. It was the reason they'd left Dallas and returned to Courtland.

She gave him one of the pain pills the doctor had prescribed and a glass of water. It wasn't long before he drifted off to sleep, but sleep wouldn't come for her. Her nerves were raw now. She placed her gun on her lap. She wanted it close by just in case. These men had found her, slipped through the Avery brothers' protection and tried to kill her for something she didn't even have or know how to find.

How could anyone find comfort in that?

She stared at the photos on the wall of Josh and a woman. It had to be his late wife. Colby said she'd been murdered right here in this cabin. He knew what it was like to lose someone he loved. So did Colby. So did she. She hated how she'd taken her cousin for granted and how she'd allowed jealousy and resentment to fester between them.

Her mind went back to the conversation she'd had with Colby. Was he right? Had she done the same thing with God? She kept expecting Him to reach down and fix everything in her life, but why should He when she'd turned her back on Him so many years ago?

Was it fair to make God prove Himself to her before she even accepted Him? It wasn't, but that didn't make reaching out to Him any easier.

She stared out the window at the darkening landscape. He'd made a beautiful country. She'd seen beautiful places and she'd seen war-torn areas of the world. She couldn't blame God for the ugliness. That was all man. That was all people.

Brooke eyed the night sky and felt a sudden desire. Dare she ask? Should she even bother to put herself out there again with Him? Would He ignore her this time when so much was at stake?

She'd done everything she could to find out who'd killed Tessa. Why not do everything possible and ask for His help? Tessa had believed in God. She'd had faith in something bigger than herself.

Brooke took a deep breath and glanced at the ceiling. "God?" Her face warmed. How silly she felt talking to the air or some invisible force she couldn't see. "God? Are You there? I really need Your help. People are after me, and I'm scared." That hurt to admit, but she pushed on. "I can't do this alone any longer." Tears pressed against her eyes and slipped through. She didn't bother wiping them away as a rush of emotion swept over her. She was tired of doing everything alone. She was ready to let someone else in, ready to trust again in someone and something besides herself. She was tired of being so angry and afraid.

She closed her eyes and heard…nothing.

There was no big revelation. In fact, there was no answer at all. If God was even listening, He wasn't responding to her.

She propped her chin on her hand and closed her eyes. Only the sounds of the night reached her ears. The soft hum of the air conditioner kicking on. Horses whinnying in the distance. Crickets chirping. Dogs barking.

A noise grabbed her attention and she jerked, horrified to realize she'd fallen asleep in the chair while waiting on some mystical revelation from God. How silly was that?

She stood and walked to the window, pressing her hand to the curtain. Everything outside the window seemed quiet and still, but her gut was telling her everything was not fine.

What was the noise that had awoken her?

She glanced at the sofa. Colby was still asleep, so it must not have been as loud as she was making it out to be. He moved in his sleep and a name escaped his lips.

"Tessa."

She closed her eyes. The pain of that word stabbed at her. She was scared, and not just of the men out to get her. She was scared of losing her heart to Colby and having it crushed. He was obviously still hung up on her cousin and saw Brooke as nothing more than a replacement for Tessa. He'd just proven that. Her face warmed thinking about that kiss this afternoon. She should never have allowed that to happen again, but it had felt so good. Being here, being with Colby, was only causing that attraction to grow. She had to get a handle on it before she wound up with a broken heart.

Brooke walked to the kitchen, poured herself a glass of milk, set it in the microwave and pressed the button. She needed something to help her relax.

Voices outside grabbed her attention.

She spun to face the front door. She hadn't imagined that. She marched toward the window, grabbing the gun she'd left on the table as she walked. It was probably only Colby's brothers. They'd promised to keep an eye on things. She was overreacting, but that didn't stop the hammering of her pulse as she peered through the curtain.

Footsteps on the porch made her backtrack nearer to the bedroom. She hid behind an open closet door, gun raised and ready just in case. Her mind was still telling her she was being silly and it was Josh coming inside to make sure everything was okay, but her gut told her differently. Unfortunately, it was rarely wrong.

The locks on the door groaned against an external force and the door opened, causing her breath to quicken. A figure stepped inside and glanced around. She saw only the shadow of his face from the glow of the light from the stove lamp. She also saw the outline of something in his hand. She grimaced. A gun. Of course, it was a gun.

She did her best to try to blend into the wall. He moved past her, pushed open the bedroom door, and checked the bathroom. She got a better look at him in the light from the room. Tall, dark hair, tattoo on his neck. It was the same man who'd attacked her at the hospital.

Timothy Mason.

He'd found her here in Courtland.

He turned and caught her eye. She had her gun raised before he could move. She had him. But instead of being concerned she'd snuck up on him, he grinned.

Anger burned through her. "What are you smiling at?"

She found out a moment later when someone grabbed her from behind, clamping his sweaty hand over her mouth. Mason took the gun from her while his accomplice dragged her through the open front door and down the porch steps. She squirmed and fought them with all her might. She couldn't go like this. She should have woken Colby when she'd heard the first sound. He would never know what had happened to her.

She tried to force her face free. At least she could scream and grab his attention. He might not be able to help her, but he would at least have an idea that something was happening to her.

She pulled her arm free and smacked the man holding her. His grip loosened, and she nearly managed to squirm free, but the other guy grabbed her legs and they carried her off together.

Hot anger pulsed through her. How had she let this happen? And how had they found her? More importantly, what could she possibly give them that would save her life? She still hadn't found Tessa's notes and documentation, and with Tessa's apartment destroyed, Brooke doubted she ever would.

"Stop!"

The men turned. Colby stood on the porch, his gun raised. He'd found her!

Her abductor shifted, and she managed to squirm free of his hand. "Colby!"

Mason dropped her feet and pulled his gun. He fired at Colby while his accomplice dragged her by her arms toward a waiting van.

Suddenly, a shot rang out and horses rounded the cabin.

"Stop!"

She heard a voice cry out on the wind and the sound of hooves near her. His brothers had arrived. They took several shots, and the man had no choice but to drop her to grab his gun and return fire. She stumbled out of the line of fire, hurrying around a bale of hay.

Someone pulled on her arm, and she screamed.

"It's me. It's Colby."

Relief flooded her, and she fell into his arms.

Mason and his accomplice hopped into a waiting van and took off. Josh and Paul rode after them in pursuit.

Colby wrapped her into his arms then pushed her away and stared into her eyes. Grief and pain filled his expression.

"I thought I'd lost you." He groaned and tugged her against him. "When I woke up and saw they had you, I thought I'd lost you for good."

"For a moment, I thought you had too," she admitted.

He pulled her into a kiss. His lips enveloped hers and she melted into his arms, struggling to catch her breath as he locked her into his embrace. She didn't want to leave this spot, didn't want this moment to end.

Unfortunately, it did.

Colby's brothers were back, and he ended the kiss and turned to them, his chest still heaving to catch his breath.

"Did you catch them?"

Paul shook his head. "We didn't. I called Josh and he's putting out a BOLO for the vehicle and diverting deputies."

"How did they get so close to the cabin?"

He grimaced. "They lured us away from it with a motorcycle rider." Anger filled his expression. "It's my fault. I thought we were doing the right thing."

"It's okay," Brooke told him. "I'm safe. Everyone is safe now."

"We'll have to watch the cabin even closer," Paul said. "I'll call Zeke, and we can form two-man teams to keep an eye out 'round the clock."

Colby nodded. He turned back to Brooke and held her hand. "Nothing else is going to happen to you. I promise."

She wished he didn't look so forlorn. "I'm fine," she assured him. He might not be able to control these attacks, but he'd been there for her each time. Funny, that was the same thing he'd said about God.

They walked toward the cabin, his arm around Brooke's shoulder. She could live like this, she thought, allowing herself to see a future in this man's arms.

Suddenly, an explosion rocked the night.

* * *

Colby was thrown backward, landing hard against the ground. The blast hurt his ears and pain radiated from his shoulder. Colby glanced up at the cabin now in a blaze. Those men had done more than try to abduct to her. They'd come with a plan B. They'd planted a bomb.

Brooke lay several feet away. He forced his legs to move. He had to check on her.

Blood was dripping from a gash on her forehead. She tried to sit up and then screamed out in pain and grabbed her neck. At least she was alive.

"Stay still," he told her. "Don't move until help arrives."

He didn't want to leave her, but she was conscious. His brothers were lying still on the ground. They'd taken the brunt of the blast and had both been thrown from their horses. One of the horses lay injured on the ground. The other had bolted away. They would have to find him to make certain he wasn't injured.

Colby stared at Josh's cabin in flames. These men had gotten close enough to do that without him knowing. He'd nearly slept through it thanks to those pain pills. Nearly slept through Brooke being abducted too.

If he hadn't woken up...

He pushed those thoughts away and tried to concentrate on his brothers.

Paul moaned in pain as he woke up, and Colby moved to him. "Lay back. Help is on the way."

"What happened?"

"The cabin exploded."

Paul grimaced in anger and then spotted Lawson. "Lawson. How is he?"

Colby checked his youngest brother. "He probably has a broken leg, but he's going to be fine. We're all okay."

Over the ringing in his ears, Colby heard voices. Several figures appeared on the path to the main house. His parents along with Bree and Shelby.

"We heard the explosion," Shelby said. She hurried to Paul and wrapped her arms around him.

"I'm okay," Paul assured her.

Bree fell to the ground beside a still unconscious Lawson. Panic filled her eyes.

His mother morphed into nurse mode. It had been twenty years since she'd worked in a hospital, but she'd retained her nursing skills. She checked Lawson over, lifting his lids to peer at his pupils. "He needs to get to the hospital."

His father, who'd knelt beside her, jumped up. "I'll get the truck."

She rushed to Paul, who waved her away. "I'm okay. I'm okay. Check on Brooke."

Colby helped his mother to her feet, but she was concerned about him too. "Are you hurt?"

"I'm fine. Just some ringing in my ears and cuts and bruises. Brooke cried out in pain when she tried to sit up."

"Hopefully, it's just whiplash." She checked Brooke's pupils. "Any blurry vision or nausea?"

"No."

"You're going to be fine, Brooke, but we need to get you all checked out at the hospital."

Colby sat beside Brooke and held her hand while his mother returned to observe Lawson.

"It's going to be okay," he told her, squeezing her hand. "It's going to be okay." Only he wasn't certain if he was saying it for her benefit or his own.

He stared at the cabin on fire. These guys had gotten close this time. Too close. Josh had lost his cabin, and his evidence board and files were gone, but thankfully, none of them had lost their lives tonight. Everything else could be replaced.

Several vehicles screeched to a stop close by. Josh and Zeke, their brother-in-law, hopped out of one and hurried over.

"What happened?" Josh demanded.

"Two men tried to grab Brooke. After they ran off, the cabin blew. They must have planted a bomb before they left."

"Is anyone hurt?" He zeroed in on Lawson, who was still unconscious on the ground.

Bree glanced up at them both, tears in her eyes. "He still hasn't come to."

"We need to get him to the hospital," their mother commanded.

Colby, Josh, Paul and Zeke all took a side, lifted Lawson and carried him to the truck. They loaded him into the back seat. Colby helped his mother inside beside Bree.

"You boys get to the hospital as soon as you can and get yourselves and Brooke checked out."

"We will, Ma," Paul assured her. "Right after we get this under control." He closed the door and tapped on the roof. The truck roared away moments later.

Colby walked over to help Brooke, but Shelby was already helping her to slowly sit up. He made his way over to where Josh and Paul stood.

Josh crossed his arms. "Someone want to tell me what happened here?"

Colby stared at the burning building.

Everyone was safe. That was all that mattered for now. But he was going to have to be even more vigilant if he hoped to keep Brooke alive.

The next morning, Colby walked through the smoldering remains of the cabin with Josh, Paul and Miles. It had taken hours to extinguish the flames, and people from all over town had come by to help.

Josh pushed a hand through his hair, and he sorted through rubbish to find anything salvageable. So far, the pile was minimal. All his photographs and belongings were gone.

Plus, all the files they'd collected and all the work Colby had done on Tessa's case had been destroyed. If this group had wanted to eliminate evidence, they'd very nearly succeeded.

"Josh, I'm sorry." Colby felt the need to apologize, but Josh stopped him.

"This isn't your fault."

It sure felt like his fault. The men who'd bombed Josh's cabin had done so because Colby hadn't captured them. If he'd done his job sooner, this might not have happened.

Miles came up beside Colby. He and his wife had arrived in town early this morning, too late to do anything except help clean up the mess that had been made. "Any word on Lawson?"

Colby nodded and turned to him. "Yeah. Dad texted earlier. Said he's awake and responding. He's going to be okay."

Miles breathed a sigh of relief. "That's good. I'm not sure we could handle any more tragedy."

"I know." He motioned toward Josh. "He hardly ever stayed here, but I know this has to hurt. After all, it's all he had left of Haley."

Miles nodded. "I'm sure you're right. Where's Brooke?"

"I moved her into the main house. She's sore, but, aside from Lawson, none of us were seriously hurt."

"That's a blessing in itself."

Yes, it was. Colby still recalled the way his heart sank when he heard her screams for help. He'd nearly lost her. He couldn't let that happen again.

"When we finish cleaning this up, I'd like to go back through your files," Miles stated. "I want to help find whoever did this, if possible."

"Thanks, but most of my files were in the cabin. I'll have to contact the FBI office and ask Olivia to send us copies." All the work he'd done on his own was gone, but he'd built off his FBI files, and could repeat that if he needed to.

He rubbed his face.

Not that those leads had gone anywhere. Their best option now was to track down the members of this group who'd targeted Brooke. Hopefully, they could lead them back to whomever hired them. That would lead them to Tessa's killer.

"Do you and Brooke need anything? Clothes, phones, toiletries? I'm assuming everything was in the cabin."

"I think our bags are still in Josh's pickup. He was supposed to bring them to us after he collected them from the wrecked SUV."

Josh picked up a photograph that was burned on the edges, but his deceased wife's face was still visible. He folded it and slipped it into his pocket, and Colby didn't miss the hitch of his breath as he did it. He'd not only lost her. Now he'd lost the home they'd shared together.

Josh turned and headed out of the rubble. "None of this is salvageable. I'm heading back to the office to follow up with my deputies on tracking down that van."

Colby watched him go. Shame filled him at seeing how broken his brother was by this attack. He would find the people who did this and make them pay.

Brooke took a few pain relievers and stretched out on the couch in the living room of the main house. It was quiet here now with the men out at the cabin scene. The rest of the family was at the hospital with Lawson. She was glad to hear he was going to be fine except for a broken leg and a slight concussion.

Shelby had loaned her a laptop, and at Colby's request, Olivia had forwarded all the information they'd collected on the case. Brooke was intent on going back through it. The answers they sought had to be in there somewhere.

Shelby was working on the porch. Brooke didn't want to disturb her, and she longed for some soft music to help her concentrate. She was sure she'd seen a pair of earbuds in the bag Cecile had dropped off with the stuff they'd collected from the SUV after the wreck.

Brooke walked over and dug through the bag. It was a hodgepodge of stuff that had belonged to her, Colby and even Tessa. She'd forgotten she'd taken some things from Tessa's desk and put them in her purse. A sharp pain stung her heart at the realization that these few belongings, along with whatever could be salvaged from her office, were all she had left of her cousin.

Brooke took out the picture from Tessa's desk, the one of Tessa and Colby at the beach, but it wasn't her cousin's face that captivated her this time. It was Colby's. She outlined his handsome face with her finger. She was getting way too attached to him. She closed her eyes and realized the truth. She'd fallen for him. Her cousin's face stared back at her, admonishing her for those feelings. She shouldn't be having them since she knew she could never truly trust Colby. She wanted to, but she was so scared.

Why can't she trust him? Why can't she take the risk?

She started to push the framed photo back into the bag but couldn't stand to part with it. She wanted to keep it with her. She turned the frame over and popped open the back. She started to pull out the photo but stopped. A small black shape was taped to the back of the frame. She fingered it, pulled it off and gasped.

It was a flash drive.

It had to be the one Tessa had hidden her documentation on. It had to be the files that proved the fraud that had gotten her killed. Her heart hammered against her chest. This was it. This was what they'd been searching for. This was what Tessa had died for.

She jammed the picture into her pocket and ran to find Colby.

She pushed open the door. Shelby stood, seeing her excitement. "What's wrong?"

"Colby. I need to see Colby."

"They're at the barn."

Brooke ran down the steps and across the field.

Colby stood outside the barn with his brothers and Cecile. He looked so beat up. They all did. Beat up and worried about Lawson. She'd been so much trouble since meeting up with Colby, but she couldn't help it. Hopefully, her discovery would make up for it all.

"Brooke? What's the matter?"

Josh and Cecile looked concerned too.

"Is everything okay?" Josh asked her.

Her hands were shaking with excitement, but she managed to hold up the flash drive. "I found it. I found it."

Colby took it from her and stared at it. Excitement brewed on his face. "Is this—?"

"It was taped inside the picture frame, the one that held that picture of you and Tessa at the beach. This has to be the information she was collecting."

"We need a computer," Colby said.

"I have one on the couch," Brooke commented. "I

was about to use it to go through those FBI files Olivia sent over."

"Let's go." Josh ran past them and into the house. Cecile followed him.

Colby pulled her in for a kiss. She soaked it up as excitement spread through them both.

"This could be the key to figuring all this out." He grabbed her hand and hurried up the steps. She went with him, her adrenaline easing the pain she'd been experiencing.

Josh had the laptop set up on the kitchen table and was powering it up. Colby pressed the flash drive into the side of it and leaned over the table. His body was tense with excitement. Brooke stood behind him just as excited. This had to be the thing that would finally burst open this case and help them to figure out who was behind Tessa's death and why. They only needed to connect Dutton to it. She prayed this would the proof that would finally do it.

She'd prayed.

She gasped, realizing what she'd done, but she couldn't help asking for God's assistance again. This evidence could have easily been left behind in the apartment and lost in the fire or left sitting on Tessa's desk, never to be discovered. They had reason to be excited.

Colby took in a breath as financial documents filled the laptop's screen. Cecile pointed out some information. "That's claims data. Charges paid by an insurance company to Healthmax using multiple provider numbers. Look, all the charges are the same. Plus, it shows the account numbers that the payments went to."

"I've gone through the accounting files hundreds of times," Colby said. "I can rattle off Healthmax's bank account numbers, and none of these are it. These payments are going to a separate bank account. If Dutton's name is on any of these accounts, we can connect him to the fraud and possibly to Tessa's murder."

Cecile searched through the files. "There could be thousands of dollars not being reported as Healthmax profits."

Colby nodded. "I need to contact Olivia and have her double-check these accounts. I'll also call the White-Collar Crime Unit. They have the original information. I'm going to call it in." He looked at Brooke. "I need to return to the office in Dallas."

"I'm coming with you. But don't you think you should email this information to Olivia just in case. We can't risk the flash drive being taken." She didn't like thinking something could happen to them on the way to Dallas, but why risk it when they didn't have to.

"That's a good idea." He quickly emailed the files to Olivia, pulled the flash drive from the laptop and looked at Josh and Cecile. "This could be the break we were looking for."

"Go," Josh told him. He tossed him a set of keys. "Take my truck. I'll let everyone know you had to leave."

"Call me with any update on Lawson."

"Don't worry. I will."

Brooke grabbed her bag and tossed it into the back seat of Josh's pickup. Colby climbed behind the wheel, started the engine and took off. They weren't losing any time. He hit the button on his phone and placed a call to Olivia, telling her to look out for the email and explaining what Brooke had found and the documentation on it.

"Call down to Martin in Healthcare Fraud and get any and all records they have sent up. I want us to hit the ground running once we arrive in Dallas."

"Will do," Olivia told him.

He ended the call, reached across the seat and took Brooke's hand. "This is it," he told her. "This is the key to getting us into Dutton's files and getting a search warrant for his office."

"Do you think this will help prove that he had my cousin killed?"

"One of these bank accounts has to show a payment for a hit man. I don't believe Dutton is the type to get his hands dirty, so he must have paid someone to murder Tessa. This is what we've been looking for all along, and this is what is going to bring John Dutton and Healthmax down once and for all." He squeezed her hand. "It's all because of you, Brooke. This is all going to happen because of you. You did this."

She couldn't help the gratitude that soared through her. It felt good to be acknowledged and seen as a partner. She was glad they were working together, glad that she'd tracked him down to help her find out who'd killed Tessa.

They'd done it together, and they weren't finished yet.

They still had to go through this evidence, figure out how it pointed to Dutton and make a connection to the extremist group. The CEO had to have been the one to hire them. If they'd hoped to protect themselves, her cousin had outwitted them. She'd gotten the better of them.

Way to go, Tessa.

She stared at Colby and the excitement on his face. They were finally going to get justice for Tessa and for the attacks against Brooke as well. This might finally be over soon.

What was next?

She thought about the kiss he'd given her. Had it been out of excitement for the breakthrough in the case or something more? They'd grown closer over the past days, and they'd been through so much. She couldn't deny her attraction to him any longer. She didn't want to. She wanted to trust that Colby Avery was a good man who wanted nothing more than to see justice prevail.

They both needed to believe it would.

NINE

Colby handed the flash drive to Olivia, who logged it into evidence. She had already copied the information to the FBI database from the email he'd sent her, but they needed to go through proper channels in order to make this discovery relevant to their legal case. Brooke needed to make a statement as to where and how she'd found it. He directed her to an interview room where one of his associates had her write down everything about how she'd found it.

While she did that, Colby returned to the conference room. He scanned the documents from the drive and only got a few pages in before he called up the legal department to start working on a search warrant for Healthmax. He also called in his buddy in the fraud unit and emailed over a snippet of what they'd found. He received a very excited response in reply.

"This is a healthcare fraud-related case," Jimmy Martin said. "I want to be in on the investigation."

Colby was more than a little irritated that they hadn't wanted to be involved sooner. Martin had buckled the moment Dutton's lawyers had come at them.

"This is still a murder investigation," Colby insisted. "I need to prove Tessa's murder is related to this fraud. Murder takes precedency over your case."

"Colby, we can work together on this, right? Share evidence?"

"I've already called for a warrant to search Dutton's home and offices."

"No problem. I'll get to work on a warrant for his bank accounts and assets." Martin's excitement was evident even over the phone.

Colby was excited the case finally had some traction. He owed it all to Tessa for gathering this…and to Brooke for finding it.

Brooke.

He couldn't believe how he'd fallen for the lovely brunette. Once they had the case wrapped up, he couldn't wait to take her in his arms and prove to her how much she meant to him.

"This time, we're not giving up until we find what we're looking for. Agreed?"

"Agreed," Martin replied. "Let me know when the warrant comes through. I'm heading toward your office."

Two hours later, the warrant was signed. Colby was anxious to get on the road and execute it. He loaded up his gear. He might not need it, but you never knew how people were going to react. Last time, Dutton had been haughty because he'd known they had little evidence. This time, he might realize he'd been undone.

He walked with Martin through the office and saw Brooke still waiting in the conference room. Her statement had been critical in obtaining the search warrant. He wanted to at least let her know what was happening. He'd been so caught up in preparing for this raid that he hadn't spoken to her in hours or kept her updated.

He went to her, and she stood, eyeing his FBI-issued vest, jacket and ball cap. "You look intimidating."

"We got the warrant to search Healthmax. We're heading there now." He reached for her hand and squeezed it. "We couldn't have done it without you, Brooke. You made this happen. We're finally going to nail Dutton for fraud and murder."

He glanced at the table and noticed the photograph of him and Tessa, the one Brooke had brought from Tessa's office. He picked it up and stared at it. He outlined her face in the photo. He was finally going to get justice for her after all these months. Guilt filled him that it had taken him this long, but it was happening now, and it was all because of Brooke.

Brooke stared up at him. Her lashes were wet with tears. Happy tears, he hoped. He wiped a stray drop away with his finger and kissed her forehead. "This is going to take a while. I'll have an agent take you to a hotel and keep watch. I'll call once we're done. Then we should talk."

She nodded and gave him a small wave goodbye. He walked away but couldn't help one last glance back at her. None of this would be happening without her involvement. He was so thankful God had sent her to him. Once this was over, he would make sure she understood how grateful he was and how much he wanted her in his life.

* * *

Brooke watched Colby walk out. She fell into her chair and pressed her hand over her face. Anguish nearly took over her control, but she did her best to hold in her emotions.

She stared at the picture on the table. Her cousin's eyes seemed to mock her. The way he'd stroked the outline of Tessa's face had been proof that Brooke had been a silly, foolish pushover. Even after all this time, he was still hung up on Tessa.

It shouldn't matter. Tessa was dead. She wasn't a rival any longer, but Brooke could never feel comfortable knowing Colby would rather be with her cousin than with her. Shame washed over her at the way she'd fawned over him. The way she'd melted at his kisses and leaned into his embraces.

She was a fool. A fool Colby wouldn't want anything to do with now they'd caught her cousin's murderer. Would she be cast aside now that his case was solved and justice had been served?

She steeled herself at the thought of his disinterest. Even worse would be knowing he really would prefer to be with her cousin. She wouldn't sit around and wait for him to decide he was through with her. She wasn't that desperate.

She allowed an agent to drive her to the hotel and clear the room for her. Once he was gone, she drew the curtains and fell onto the bed. Sobs racked her body, and she allowed them to come. She needed that release to be able to do what her heart was begging her not to do. She needed to end things with Colby before he could do the same.

She'd put herself out there once again only to have her heart broken. For him, everything led back to Tessa. Colby would never see her as more than a replacement for her cousin.

Anger pulsed through her. Anger that she'd allowed herself to, once again, have her heart broken.

Never again.

Her future that had once seemed so bright only a few hours ago, now looked bleak again. There was only one person she could trust in life—herself. It was about time she got used to it. She was truly alone.

Colby and the other agents pulled up to the Healthmax suite and spread out. He handed the warrant over to the receptionist, who immediately phoned Dutton. He arrived within moments, glanced at the warrant, at Colby, and sighed. "I'm phoning my attorney."

"That's a good idea. Why don't you do that?" Colby motioned toward a conference room. "Use that phone and remain in there while we conduct our search. I'm posting a guard to make certain you don't try to leave. I'd also like you to notify your department heads that we're going to search and take any and all information we need pursuant to the warrant."

Dutton nodded at the receptionist. "Let everyone know to cooperate." She picked up the phone and started making calls. He turned back to Colby. "And don't worry. I'm not planning on going anywhere. Gather whatever evidence you want. I have nothing to hide."

He marched into the conference room and picked up a phone. His defenses were up, but that was to be expected when the FBI marched full-force into your business.

Colby posted a guard by the door, instructing him that Dutton's lawyer could enter, but Dutton wasn't allowed to leave the room until they'd finished their sweep. Colby would have questions Dutton would need to answer afterward.

He left the other agents to do their jobs while he and Greg went upstairs to Dutton's office. It was tidy and low-key. Nothing extravagant like he'd expected. A row of photographs on the desk showed his wife and children. He was putting forth the good guy image to a tee.

Colby started on the cabinets while Greg took the desk. He'd searched only a few minutes when Greg called to him.

He turned and spotted his boss holding up a cell phone. "Look what I found."

Colby recognized the cell phone cover with the inspirational quote the moment he saw it. The phone was dead, so they would need to charge it for confirmation, but he knew this was Tessa's missing cell phone. He slipped it into an evidence bag and sighed as Greg signed and labeled it.

This was all the evidence they needed to link John Dutton to Tessa's murder.

"We did it, Brooke. We arrested Dutton." Colby's voice over the phone held such excitement. Brooke wished she could match it, but she'd spent the past hours doing her best to pull herself together and make plans. She couldn't manage excitement when her world was falling apart around her.

"Finally, we're going to get justice for what he did to your cousin."

She was glad he'd found the person responsible for Tessa's murder, but the determination in his voice, the relief, stung her again. Tessa was all he thought about these days. Brooke had made up her mind. She wasn't going to be second best to anyone, even her dead cousin.

"I'm heading to the hotel. I need to interrogate Dutton, but he can stew for a while. I want to see you first."

She told him she would be there and then ended the call, glad he'd called first. She needed time to wash her face and clean herself up. Ashamed of herself for losing her heart to this man, she wouldn't further humiliate herself by letting him see just how far she'd fallen.

She jumped when the knock on the door came. Now that he was there, she wasn't sure she was strong enough to go through with it. There was a very real chance she might melt the moment he turned those blue eyes her way.

No. She had to remain strong. This was the right thing to do. The case was over. Tessa's murder had been solved. She'd done what she'd come to do. It was time to remove herself from this situation before her heart took any more beatings. She had to end it with him before he could do it to her.

Brooke smoothed her hair and steeled herself with a deep breath. When she opened the door, Colby was leaning against the doorway, his eyes glistening with exhilaration. Before she could speak, he pulled her into an embrace and kissed her. She fought at first and then gave in to the sensation of being in his arms. One last kiss. One last embrace. One last scent of his leathery cologne. It was all she would allow herself.

He ended the kiss and held her face. "We did it. We caught him, Tessa."

She stiffened at the name he'd called her. Anger and indignation soared through her.

He didn't seem to notice his slip of the tongue or her reaction to it. "Finally, he'll answer for what he's done."

She wiped the kiss from her lips. She closed the door and fisted her hands as she fought to control her composure. "I'm happy, of course. I hope he spends a long time in jail thinking about what he did to my cousin. I'll try to make it back to town for the trial."

He turned to her and shot her a glance, his smile fading a bit. "What do you mean by that?"

She steadied herself for what was to come. It wouldn't be easy, but it was the right thing to do. "I'm leaving town. I've done what I came here to do. It's time for me to move on."

His eyes narrowed, a mixture of confusion and impending dread in his expression. "What are you talking about? Where are you going?"

"Back to the army."

"But I thought you were done with that life? You said—"

"I know what I said, but I was wrong." She folded her arms to keep herself strong. This was more difficult than she'd imagined. "The army is all I know. It's where I belong."

"Brooke, wait a minute. We should talk about this."

"There's really nothing to talk about, Colby. I've made up my mind."

"But what about… I mean what about…" His face reddened a bit. "What about us? I thought we had something."

He sounded so sincere and heartbroken that she nearly caved. Then she remembered the way he'd outlined Tessa's face on the photograph. She'd done the same to his and understood the meaning behind such a gesture.

"There's no us, Colby. There can never be. It's obvious to me that you're still hung up on my cousin." She turned away from him as tears welled up in her eyes. She wouldn't cry in front of him.

"What are you talking about?" He sounded angry, frustrated. She didn't try to explain, and after several moments of not getting a response, he gave a heavy sigh. "Please, don't do this," he whispered, the anguish in his voice clear.

"This just isn't going to work, Colby. You—you're in love with a memory, and I won't be a replacement for her."

"You're not. I promise you're not."

"You told me yourself you were in love with Tessa."

"Tessa is dead."

"And I'm alive. I won't be your second choice just because she's not here." She'd spent her life being in Tessa's shadow. Maybe they looked alike, but that was where their similarities ended. If Colby was expecting her to be Tessa, he would eventually be disappointed and grow to resent her. She didn't think her heart could survive that. It was better to push him away now than be heartbroken once she'd given her heart to him fully.

"You're wrong," he told her. "I don't see you as a replacement for Tessa. Yes, I cared for her. It might have been something serious, but we never got that chance to find out because she gave up on us. She ended it, Brooke. She wasn't strong enough to fight for us. I don't blame her. Not everyone is built to be the wife of a law enforcement officer. I understood that. But you are not a replacement for Tessa. You have qualities that she never did. You're strong and determined. I've never met a woman as determined as you. You know what you want and you go after it with gusto and without fear. And you're beautiful, not because of how you look, but because of your determination and kindness. You are more than a look-alike for her. I never have to wonder where I stand with you because you're open and generous and kind in spirit. Brooke, I'm begging you, please don't give up on us."

"My concerns are not trivial."

"I didn't mean to imply they were." He took her by the shoulders and turned her to face him. "But, Brooke, I love you."

His proclamation of love nearly did her in. She loved him too. So much. But she still wasn't sure about his feelings for her. How could she ever be certain he didn't see Tessa every time he looked at her?

She couldn't.

And she couldn't risk her heart over it either.

"I'm sorry, Colby, but I can't do this." She walked to the door and opened it. "Once I finish going through and packing up whatever is left of Tessa's office, I'm leaving Dallas for good."

He stared at her for several moments. She avoided his eyes, but felt his pleading stares. She couldn't falter. She had to remain strong. She couldn't fall apart until he was gone.

Finally, he moved toward the door, but he stopped before crossing the threshold. He leaned down close, so close that she could feel his breath on her cheek as he whispered to her. "I won't give up on you, Brooke."

He walked out of the room and down the hall. She closed the door, but the moment he was gone, the sobs started, and these she couldn't push back. They came fierce and demanding. She fell onto the bed, covered her face with her hands and let them come.

Colby slammed a file on the table where John Dutton sat handcuffed in the FBI interrogation room. It gave him satisfaction to see this man in cuffs finally, but that satisfaction didn't change the fact that he was heartbroken over the situation with Brooke. He tried his best to concentrate on the matter at hand, but it was hard when all he could think about was finding a way to keep her from leaving.

He slid the bagged cell phone across the table for Dutton to see. Instead of recognition, confusion and annoyance clouded his expression. "What is this?"

"We found this hidden inside your desk at your office at Healthmax. It belonged to Dr. Tessa Morgan."

His eyes widened. He knew the relevance of that. His face hardened. "I've never seen this before."

"That's not going to cut it, Dutton. This cell phone links you to her murder. She was going to expose your fraudulent operation, so you and your extremist buddies had her killed."

"Extremist buddies? What are you talking about?"

"I'm talking about the Freedom from Government Interference, a radicalized anti-government extremist group. They targeted Brooke to try to find the documentation Tessa uncovered proving Healthmax's fraudulent behavior. Are you going to deny hiring them to kill her?"

He stiffened and leaned back in his seat. "I haven't committed any fraud, Agent, and I don't know anything about any extremist group. You have nothing to tie me to them."

"This is the only thing I need," Colby insisted. "Even if I can't tie you to the organization, I can tie you to Tessa's murder through this. You murdered her and then you took this from her."

"I had nothing to do with Dr. Morgan's death. I've already told you, I was at home the night she was killed. My wife can verify I was home the entire night."

"Your wife's alibi isn't going to save you, Dutton. Do you think she's still going to support you once she learns about this cell phone? I've got agents searching your house and cars as we speak. We'll find something else to convince her you're not worthy of her devotion."

"You'll find nothing because I haven't done anything."

A buzz of Colby's cell phone grabbed his attention. He glanced at it. Olivia wanted to see him outside. "I'll be back." He gathered up his files and Tessa's cell phone and stepped out of the room.

Olivia smiled up at him. "You're going to love me for this." She handed him a file. He opened it to find pages listing accounts with large sums of money flowing through them, all bearing Dutton's name.

"It looks like he's been funneling money through these accounts. Many of them are closed, but there's still several thousand left in one account. We called in a forensic accountant who claims it looks like most of the money has been funneled offshore, but these account all bear Dutton's name. He can't claim not to know about this. Plus, we've found an email sent to an anonymous source. It doesn't specify he was looking for a hit man, but it certainly looks like that's what he was doing."

No way could Dutton dispute this evidence. "This is good. Thanks for finding it."

She waved away his thanks. "Just doing my job."

And she was good at her job. Colby was glad to have her on his team. With a re-energized bounce in his step, Colby walked back into the interrogation room. He steadied himself for this confrontation. Dutton might still not want to cop to this, but the evidence was enough to convict him even without a confession. Colby still wanted one. He wanted Dutton to confess that he'd ordered the hit on Tessa. It was the least he owed her for a life taken.

He sat, leaned back in his chair and opened the file. Dutton watched him and waited for him to speak, but he kept silent. He wanted the man to stew for a few minutes.

"What is it?" Dutton finally asked him. "What else do you want to know? I'm innocent. You're looking in the wrong place."

Colby put the open file on the table and slid it over so Dutton could see the bank account information bearing his name. "If you're so innocent, how do you explain these?"

The CEO glanced at the file. His eyes widened and he fumbled for words. Colby took notice. He looked stunned...but was it because he'd been found out or because he was surprised to see the accounts?

"I don't know anything about these."

Colby had seen guilty men before. He'd looked them in the eye and seen their arrogance and haughtiness. Dutton showed no signs of either. His surprise seemed genuine. Moments later, it turned to outrage and indignation.

"Someone is setting me up. You have to believe me. I have two mortgages. I'm upside down on my car lease. I just had to tell my daughter she can't take ballet lessons because we can't afford them. Why would I live this way if I have access to this kind of money?"

"Somehow you've gotten entangled with this group of radical extremists. Maybe they're forcing you to do this and hand over the money. If that's what is happening, you can tell me. We can protect you and your family."

"That's not what's happening. I'm telling you, Agent Avery, I don't know anything about any of this. Someone is setting me up."

His voice and body language dripped with fear and uncertainty. That couldn't be faked. Colby's instincts were on high alert. Something wasn't feeling right about any of this.

He gathered the files and walked out. Olivia had been watching from the window. She turned to him. "What do you think?"

He shook his head. "I'm not sure."

"Not sure how to get him to confess?"

He looked at her and then at Dutton through the glass. The man had his head in his hands and his body was stiff with worry. "I'm not sure we've got the right person in custody."

Olivia gave him an incredulous look. "You don't really believe his story about being set up, do you?"

"I don't know what to think right now. I've seen guilty men. He's not acting like one."

"You can't deny the evidence against him, Colby. We have him dead to rights."

"I know. I know." He rubbed his face, trying to wipe away the suspicion gnawing through his gut. "I can't deny my instincts either, and this feels wrong. I've interrogated hundreds of people and never doubted the evidence against them. But Dutton…? Dutton's behavior is making me second-guess everything I know about this case. This man is either an incredible actor or…" He couldn't even bring himself to say the words, to give up the fight he'd been raging for over four months, ever since Tessa's body had been found.

Olivia wasn't going to let him off the hook that easily. She nudged him on. "Or?"

"Or he's innocent." He sighed and handed her back the file. "Let's double-check everything."

Suddenly, losing Brooke wasn't his only problem.

Brooke arranged for the FBI agent Colby had stationed guarding her door to drive her to get another rental car and then she relieved him of duty. What was the point now that John Dutton was in custody and they had the evidence they needed against him?

Once on her own, she headed to the hospital to finish cleaning out Tessa's office before leaving town for good.

Like her apartment, Tessa's office had been set ablaze. The fire had been extinguished quickly but much of what was left would have to be trashed. She loaded a stack of books that had survived the fire with only singed pages into a box, along with a few odds and ends. The director had assured her the maintenance staff would take care of cleaning up whatever was left.

"Hi, Brooke. Do you have a minute?"

Brooke looked up to see Sheila, the woman from Healthmax that her cousin had befriended, standing in the doorway. She chewed on her lip and glanced around nervously. She was obviously on edge, so Brooke couldn't say no. "Sure. Come on in."

But instead of doing so Sheila leaned against the doorframe. "I guess you know about Mr. Dutton being arrested."

Sheila's demeanor made sense now. Her company had been turned upside down by John Dutton's arrest. The young woman was probably wondering if she would still have a job tomorrow. "Yes, I know."

"Is it true what they're saying? Did he kill Dr. Morgan?"

"It certainly looks that way. The FBI found her cell phone in his desk."

"I can't believe it. I've been working for a murderer all this time. I don't know what's going to happen to us now. The entire office is in a tizzy. I honestly don't know if I should be at my desk working or just go home until someone tells me if we're still in business."

"I'm sure Mr. Dutton's lawyers will have something to say about that. The hospital as well. But he's going to prison for a long, long time for what he did."

"You believe he killed your cousin."

"I believe it, and Colby and the FBI will make certain he pays for what he did. Tying him to the health-care fraud makes it a federal case."

Sheila chewed on her lip again. There was something about her demeanor that Brooke couldn't identify. She was worried about something, and it wasn't merely about whether or not she still had a job. Was she worried about being swept up in the fraud investigation?

"I don't want you to worry, Sheila," Brooke told her. "I'm sure, whatever happens, you're going to be fine. John Dutton can't hurt anyone any longer. The FBI will make certain of that."

"I see you're busy clearing out her stuff. I won't keep you. I just wanted to tell you before you left how much

I really liked Tessa. She was always nice to me, even when she cut her hand and needed stitches, she took time out to talk to me. Not everyone would be that nice."

Brooke did her best to maintain a straight face, but Sheila's words rocked her. She'd just admitted to seeing Tessa on the night she'd died. She was almost certain Sheila had previously claimed she hadn't seen Tessa for several days prior to her murder.

She couldn't stop the bite in her voice when she responded. "Yes, Tessa was an amazing person, a talented physician and an incredible cousin. She didn't deserve to be murdered and dumped on the side of the road."

Sheila hesitated only for a brief second before giving a nod of agreement. She moved toward the door. "Well, I'll let you get back to work."

Brooke followed her to the door and watched her disappear down the corridor. Her heart was racing at this new development. She took a deep breath and tried to calm down. She was probably only misremembering, but she would run it past Colby just to be sure before she left town.

She picked up the box of Tessa's belongings and carried it outside to the parking garage. Her phone rang as she walked. Colby. He'd tried phoning her several times throughout the day, but she'd let the calls all go unanswered. She didn't want to rehash their conversation from yesterday. She wasn't sure she was strong enough for that. But she needed to tell him about her suspicions about Sheila, so she answered this call.

"You finally answered. Does that mean you're ready to talk?"

She heard the frustration—and hope—in his voice, and she hated the way her chest fluttered in response. "No. I've made my decision, Colby. I only picked up because I just had an odd encounter with Sheila Wilkinson."

"Sheila Wilkinson? The woman from Healthmax? Are you at the hospital? Where's Aaron?"

"He took me to get a rental car and then I told him to go. I don't need protection any longer. I was just cleaning out the rest of Tessa's belongings from her office and then I'm leaving town."

He growled, his frustration at her actions evident. But she hadn't answered his call to get into another disagreement. "Colby, forget about that. Listen to me. Sheila mentioned something about seeing Tessa the night she had to get stitches in her hand. That was the same night she was killed, wasn't it?"

"It was the same night. The staff in the ER were the last ones to see her alive."

"It might be nothing, but I'm sure Sheila told me previously that she hadn't seen Tessa for days before the murder."

"You're right. She did say that."

"Is it possible she was involved in this along with Dutton? Has he mentioned her?"

"He hasn't said anything. He still insists he's done nothing wrong and that he's being set up." He gave a weary sigh. "To be honest, Brooke, I'm starting to believe his story. It's just too crazy not to be true. Plus, I've seen guilty men. Dutton doesn't strike me that way. Either he's a very good liar or—"

"Or he's innocent," she finished.

He clicked a pen. "Let me do some digging into Sheila. Maybe there's more to this story than we've uncovered so far. I'll call you back…that is, assuming you'll take the call."

She sighed, pulled out her key fob, pressed it to unlock the car and hit the trunk button. It seemed there might be more to Tessa's murder case than they'd thought, so she needed to stay in contact with Colby. "I'll answer as long as we keep the conversation about the case and noth—"

Quick footsteps behind her caused her to turn. Sheila was behind her, lifting what looked like a tire iron over her head and swinging it hard at her. Brooke screamed and dropped her phone, raising her arms to protect herself from the blow. The iron clipped the side of her head, and she lost her breath as pain coursed through her. From the ground, she heard Colby's voice on the phone demanding to know what was happening. Stars filled her vision as she stumbled backward. Sheila shoved her into the open trunk.

She managed to call out for help as Sheila slammed the trunk lid closed and darkness surrounded her.

TEN

"Brooke!"

Colby leaped to his feet and grabbed his keys off his desk. He hurried into the conference room and found Olivia. "Call the hospital and get the security feeds for the parking garage. Then call the police and get security video for the surrounding area. And have the police and forensic team meet me there."

She turned to him, her eyes wide with surprise. "What's happened?"

Greg hurried down the hall. "What's happening?"

"I think Brooke has been kidnapped."

"What? By whom? We have Dutton in custody."

This proved his intuition was probably right. Dutton wasn't behind this. They hadn't found anything in his background check that indicated he had any ties with any radical groups, especially those who targeted the American government. And if that wasn't true, then he might be innocent of the fraud and of having Tessa murdered.

"That's what I intend to find out."

He hurried down the stairs and out of the building before hopping into his SUV, then turned on the siren and took off, whizzing in and out of traffic as he headed for the hospital. His phone was still connected to Brooke's. She must have dropped it when she was attacked. He didn't have the heart to end the call...not until he knew for certain she wasn't on the other side needing to hear his voice. He didn't think she was. He'd heard her cry out and then what had sounded like car doors and a vehicle driving away. But was Brooke with them? Or unconscious on the ground? His gut said she was gone. He didn't hear any movement on the other end of the call, but he wasn't taking any chances until he knew for certain.

His phone rang. Olivia. He didn't want to click off Brooke's call, but he needed whatever information Olivia had to give him. He hit the answer key. Even if the other call dropped, he was nearly to the hospital. "What do you have?"

"I was able to tap into the hospital security feeds. It looks like someone attacked her from behind and shoved her into the trunk of her rental car. I've already contacted the rental company to turn on the GPS. I'll let you know once I get those coordinates. I've got security and a forensics team en route."

He thanked Olivia and ended the call. Only dead air greeted him on the other line. His worst fear was realized. Brooke wasn't there. She'd been taken.

He swallowed hard. *God, please help me find her.* He couldn't lose her. Not now when he'd finally been able to admit he loved her.

He roared into the parking garage, stopping when he spotted a group of security personnel blocking off an area. He screeched to a halt and got out. The chief of security hurried toward him.

"What do we have?" Colby asked him, flashing his badge.

"She was definitely taken. I've already forwarded all of our security footage to your analyst. I've also cordoned off the area. No one has touched anything."

Colby pushed through a group of security and local police. He glanced at the area they'd blocked off. The first thing he spotted was the cell phone, Brooke's cell phone, lying on the ground.

The other items scattered on the ground included an overturned box, books, trinkets and photographs. She'd been packing up Tessa's office and carrying this box out to her car when she was grabbed. She'd been surprised. He knew that from being on the phone with her. Wherever she was, she was in trouble.

God, please keep her safe until I can get to her.

He pulled out his phone and called Josh, his hands shaking as he dialed the number. "Brooke has been taken," he said when Josh answered.

Josh took in a deep breath. "Colby, I'm sorry. Was it Dutton? I thought you had him in custody."

"I do. He isn't responsible for this."

"You think it's the people he has working for him?"

"I don't think this has anything to do with Dutton. I spent all afternoon interrogating him. He's being set up to take the fall for the fraud and murder. I want to do a deep dive into everyone in Tessa's life and see if we can tie someone to the radical group. We know they were after her. Somehow, this all fits together."

"We'll start working on our end and send whatever we find to the FBI offices."

"Thanks, Josh."

He ended the call and then remembered Brooke's suspicion about Sheila and called Olivia. "I need you to look into Sheila Wilkinson, the claims manager at Healthmax. Brooke thought she might have lied about seeing Tessa the night she died."

The noise of Olivia's typing filtered through the phone. "I'm looking at the security video. The person who attacked her was wearing dark clothes and a ball cap but the build might be a woman's. I'll check her out."

"Thanks, Olivia." He slipped his phone back into his pocket and stared at the scene where Brooke's rental car used to be. He was empty without her. He couldn't lose her, not now, when he'd just started to live again.

He needed to get her back…even if it was just long enough to tell her how much he loved her.

The hammering in her head was the first thing Brooke knew when she awoke. The next was that she was tied to a chair. Voices and movement floated to her. She blinked several times to try to force her eyes to focus. Two people, a man and woman, were in the next room. They were running around, cramming clothes from a dresser into suitcases on the bed. Suddenly, everything came rolling back to her.

Sheila had hit her over the head and stuffed her into

the trunk of her own rental car. Now, it seemed Sheila and her partner were frantic to get away from wherever they were.

She glanced around. She was in what looked like a small living room. To her left was a kitchen. To her right, a bedroom. A window with sheer curtains showed outside. She saw a dirt driveway, a lot of grass and trees, and no neighbors close by. They were obviously in the country. But where?

Brooke squirmed and pulled at the duct tape that bound her. She needed to break free and get away from Sheila. She wasn't exactly sure what was happening, but given their last conversation, Sheila had possibly been involved in Tessa's murder. Brooke wasn't in any hurry to join her cousin, but the duct tape they'd bound her hands and legs with wasn't budging.

Sheila must have heard her moving around because she turned from the bedroom and approached Brooke. "You're awake." The woman still looked edgy and ready to spring on her at any moment.

"Wha-what are you doing? Why did you hit me?"

She folded her arms over her chest and looked indignant. "I knew you were on to me the moment I left Tessa's office. I knew I'd said the wrong thing about Tessa's hand the moment I said it. It was a rookie mistake. I was only trying to find out where you were on the investigation. Ross was furious at me for blowing it like that. He keeps telling me I'm too impulsive. I act before thinking about the consequences."

She followed Sheila's gaze to the bedroom and saw the other person—a man, obviously Ross, the boyfriend

Sheila had mentioned—pick up a rifle from the corner of the room and turn to watch her. Unlike Sheila, his demeanor held no edginess. He was calm and composed, a combination that terrified her even more than Sheila's edginess.

These two had killed Tessa. She was certain of it.

"You lied about seeing her the day she was murdered. You saw her. Did you kill her?"

Sheila didn't answer, at least not right away. "Tessa was a problem for us. Are you going to be a problem too, Brooke?"

She should remain quiet and not provoke them, but she couldn't stop the anguished cry that escaped her lips. "Why did you have to kill her? She was a good person."

Sheila's face hardened. She propped her hands on her hips defiantly. "She was going to turn us in to her FBI boyfriend. We couldn't risk that."

"You didn't have to kill her. You could have closed up shop and moved on, taken your scheme to another town."

"It wasn't just about the money, Brooke. She was on to us. We had to protect ourselves. We couldn't let Tessa bring the FBI down on our group."

"What group? What are you talking about?" She didn't understand at first, but then her head cleared and she connected the dots. The extremist group that had been targeting her. Sheila and Ross were members of FGI. "You're one of them? You're a part of that group planning attacks against the government?"

"How do you think we fund those operations? Our

little scam at Healthmax brought us in hundreds of thousands of dollars that all went toward the mission."

"And what mission is that?"

"To fight against government tyranny. Our so-called government takes and takes from its citizens and uses what they've taken against us. They steal from us. Lie to us. Tax businesses into bankruptcy while ignoring the health and welfare of its most oppressed citizens."

Sheila's rant sounded like something right out of the conspiracist's playbook. She didn't know if Sheila was a true believer or just caught up in the movement for another reason. It didn't matter what Sheila's beliefs were. She'd used them to justify murder, kidnapping and fraud.

"So Dutton had nothing to do with this? It was you and Ross this whole time?"

Sheila gave an amused smile that turned her face from sweet and innocent to bitter and ugly. "He was an easy patsy. When he made me head of the billing department, it gave me the opportunity to control which reports he saw and which ones he didn't. We funneled money from those accounts to help fund our mission. And after Tessa's death, when you and that FBI agent started sniffing around, Ross came up with the idea to use his computer skills to create bank accounts, phony emails and documents that all led back to Dutton."

But it hadn't been only the bank accounts that had connected Dutton to Tessa's murder. "And Tessa's phone?"

"Planted in his office for effect. It was a nice cover-up, don't you think?"

"What I think is that you're both going to jail for a very long time."

"First, they have to catch us, and having you as a hostage will help ensure that doesn't happen."

Ross called to Sheila. "Stop blabbering and help me load the car."

Sheila started to head back to the bedroom.

"What are you going to do to me?" Brooke asked her. They'd kept her alive as a hostage, so they must want something else from her.

"I'll let Marcus decide that."

"Who's Marcus?"

"The head of our group. He'll know what to do with you."

She didn't like the sound of that. Marcus was obviously in charge, and she didn't relish being treated like a bargaining chip, especially since she knew the FBI didn't barter with terrorists, even the homegrown kind.

Sheila walked into the bedroom. Ross grabbed her arm and dug in. Brooke saw Sheila squirm. He got in her face and, although he was talking too low for Brooke to hear what he was saying, they both kept casting glances at her. Ross's face was terrifying.

He ended their conversation by backhanding Sheila. She fell sideways onto the bed while he stormed out through the front screen door. Sheila clasped a hand over her cheek, which even Brooke could see from a distance was red. Sheila pulled herself up and resumed packing.

What terrible thing had happened to Sheila to cause her to join a group like this? She seemed like a perfectly normal young woman. Sheila must have been roped into this through her relationship with Ross. He looked scary, but girls sometimes liked the bad-boy type. She was living proof of that. Jack had indeed been a bad boy, even if she hadn't realized it at first. In a way, she and Sheila shared something that few women could understand. They'd both been used and abused by the men who were supposed to love them.

If Brooke could appeal to Sheila in that context, maybe they could both get out of this unscathed. With Ross still outside at the car, now was her chance. "He shouldn't have done that to you. You didn't deserve to be hit."

Sheila stopped folding a shirt momentarily and then started again. "That's none of your business."

"No one should ever be allowed to hit you, Sheila. Is that the kind of organization this is? Where men get to go around hitting women and killing them?"

"He just lost his temper. He didn't mean to do it."

"That's what they all say. I'll bet he's been violent before, hasn't he?"

Sheila didn't turn around, but Brooke could tell she was uncomfortable by the slouch of her shoulders.

"Has he hurt you before, Sheila? Is that why you stay with him? Is that how you got pulled into this? You don't have to be afraid. Colby and the FBI can help you. We can get you out of here. They can probably even give you protection and a new life. A life where no one hits you and you don't have to be afraid."

"I said shut up." Her shoulders were shaking with emotions. Brooke was getting to her.

"Sheila, listen to me. This isn't your fault. Ross is a violent man."

"You don't know what you're talking about."

"He hits you. He probably killed Tessa, and he's going to kill us both. We have to escape from him before it's too late."

Sheila spun around, ran at Brooke and punched her hard enough to knock the chair she was tied to over. Brooke landed with a thud against the hardwood floor. Pain burst through her, but she couldn't catch her breath to cry out for several moments.

Sheila stood over her screaming, her eyes wild. "You don't know what you're talking about! Ross hasn't killed anyone! I did it! I killed Tessa! It was me!"

Brooke fought to catch her breath. Her jaw ached where Sheila had hit her. The fall plus the revelation that Sheila had murdered her cousin had pain ripping through her body. She wanted to shout out, but all she could do was sob. If Sheila had been the one to kill Tessa, then Brooke was in real trouble.

"Why did you do that?" Brooke asked.

Sheila's eyes widened. Her color paled and she bit her lip. Brooke could see that she hadn't meant to confess.

Sheila started pacing, her hands twisting frantically. "When she started asking questions, Ross sent me to make friends with her, to get close to her and find out what she knew. She told me she suspected there was fraud going on at Healthmax and that she was contacting the FBI. I panicked. I didn't know what to do. I tried to tell her it was only billing errors, but she didn't believe me. So I tried a different approach.

"I offered her money. I offered her a lot of money to keep quiet, but she refused. I don't think she even knew I was involved until that moment. Her whole expression changed when she realized I was a part of it. I knew then that our plan was in trouble. She wasn't going to keep her big mouth shut. I couldn't have her bringing the FBI sniffing around. She was going to tie us back to the FGI, and I couldn't let that happen."

"So you killed her?"

"I picked up a brick from the ground, and I hit her over the head with it. I didn't know what else to do to stop her."

Brooke closed her eyes. Sheila's confession hadn't brought her the closure she'd thought it would. Sheila had acted out of fear in a moment of panic. That, she might be able to understand, but dumping Tessa's body? That was too much. "You left her on the side of the road like a piece of garbage." Anger raged through her. "You didn't have to do that. She was a person. A good person. She was my family."

"She was a liability. And so are you." Sheila walked away, shoving open the door and walking outside to talk to Ross. The screen door slammed shut, the sound echoing the heartache bouncing through Brooke.

She had no way to wipe the tears from her eyes and she didn't care to. She'd finally gotten the answers to who had killed Tessa, and it didn't make her feel any better. Tessa had died because of rage and anger, to fuel the radical agenda of a group of angry, horrible people.

Brooke wanted to kick and rail at the unfairness of it all. She stomped her foot and was surprised when it moved. The chair had broken and the tape around her foot must have loosened when Sheila knocked her over. She moved her foot around and managed to pull it free. Success! She then did the same with her other foot and her hands until the tape gave enough for her to pull it off.

Sheila and Ross were still outside, talking and pacing in front of a car, unaware that she'd broken free. She had to act quickly if she had any hope of escaping.

She stood and searched for a telephone. If she could phone Colby, and he could somehow pinpoint her location, that would be ideal. Only she didn't see a telephone anywhere. Ross was on his cell phone, but she didn't see one that might belong to Sheila lying around.

Plan B.

She glanced into the kitchen, hoping to see a back door. If there had ever been one, it was closed up now. Who didn't have a back door in their kitchen? She would have to go out the window then. She walked to a rear-facing window and pushed it open, praying it didn't squeak. She breathed a sigh of relief when it opened far enough for her to slip through without alerting Sheila and Ross. The grass beneath the window was soft enough to break her fall. She peeked back through the window. They weren't on to her yet.

She took off running. Away from the house. Away from Sheila and Ross. She needed to find another house or a road where she could flag down a car for help. She wouldn't stop running until she did.

Sheila's scream echoed through the air. "She's escaping!"

She'd been discovered! A commotion broke out behind her, but Brooke didn't stop to look back. She kept going, pushing forward. If they captured her again, she was going to die. They were never going to let her live, not after what Sheila had revealed to her.

"Stop now!" Ross's voice echoed through the air, and then the sound of a gun firing behind her caused her to scream and stumble. She straightened and kept going. Either he'd missed her or he'd shot high to scare her. Whatever the reason she hadn't been hit, she had to put some distance between them before he fired again.

She spotted a bridge ahead of her and ran toward it. If she could get across, she might find a road or a neighbor who would help her. A car appeared on the other side. Hope welled up inside her until the car stopped and Sheila hopped out.

Brooke gripped the rail of the bridge. Sheila didn't appear to have a gun. She could probably fight her way past her if she had to, but the sound of Ross closing the distance between them ended her plans. He grabbed her by the arm and jammed his gun into her ribs.

"Did you think that was smart?" he demanded. "Don't do that again." His hot, heavy breath against her neck revolted her, and a sad truth set in. She was going to die at the hands of these two or possibly their leader, Marcus, whoever he was.

Ross shoved her toward the car. Sheila opened the back door, and Ross pushed Brooke into the back seat. He handed the gun to Sheila, and she held it on Brooke as he slid behind the wheel and drove back to the house.

Sheila gave her an angry glare. "You didn't really think you could get away, did you?"

Tears slipped down Brooke's cheek. She didn't bother to wipe them away. She wasn't going to make it out of this alive. She'd come to find answers about her cousin. She'd gotten answers, but now she was going to die like Tessa.

Worst of all, she was going to die with Colby thinking she hated him. He'd said he loved her, and she'd pushed him away. That caused the tears to slip through faster. She'd let some silly thing like his affection for her cousin get between them. Why had she been so afraid to admit her feelings to him? She'd been so afraid of having her heart broken. It seemed silly to her now. She loved him. She could admit that now when it was too late to tell him so.

Would he blame himself for her death the way he blamed himself for Tessa's? She hoped not, but she knew him well enough now to know he would. He was a protector by nature, and he hadn't been able to protect Tessa from the evil of the world. He would feel the same way about Brooke's death. She only hoped, she prayed, he would figure out who was behind this, and bring Sheila, Ross and the entire organization to justice.

Colby paced in front of the big screen in the FBI tech room. The computer was running multiple programs at once, but they weren't working fast enough for him.

"What's happening?" Greg asked, strolling into the room.

"I've got deep-dive background checks running on

all the workers at Healthmax, including John Dutton. It doesn't look like he's involved in any way I can tell."

"Have we gotten that security footage yet?"

"Yes." He motioned for Olivia to pull it up. On the big screen was an image of Brooke walking to her car carrying the box of Tessa's belongings. Moments later, a figure came up behind her and hit her over the head. She dropped the box and her phone. The woman—he was certain it was a woman—shoved her into the trunk before closing it, hopping into her rental car and driving away.

It was a vicious attack to watch, especially when his blood was boiling.

"Have we located the car?" Greg asked.

Olivia answered. "Yes. We located it through GPS. It was abandoned on the side of the road six miles from the hospital."

"What about this woman? Have we identified her yet?"

Colby stopped the video and zeroed in on the woman's profile. He clicked a few buttons. "We believe her name is Sheila Wilkinson. She works at Healthmax and claimed to be friends with Tessa. Brooke was telling me as we spoke on the phone that she thought Sheila had lied about not seeing Tessa the night she died. The next thing I knew, she was being attacked."

"Have you found any connections between this Sheila and the extremist group?"

"Nothing yet," Olivia responded. "We think she may be working with a partner. Tessa was a tall woman, and moving a dead body takes lots of muscle. She would have had a difficult time moving Tessa's body without help or without someone seeing. She has to be working with another person."

Greg turned to Colby. "Have you tried talking to Dutton? Maybe he can give you some insight into Sheila."

"That's a good idea." Colby couldn't believe he hadn't thought about that. Dutton could still be of use to them even if it appeared he hadn't known what was going on right under his nose at his own company.

Colby phoned down to the holding area and had Dutton moved to the interview room. He was there waiting when Colby arrived.

He tossed Sheila's file onto the table along with the image of her after she'd clubbed Brooke. "Sheila Wilkinson. Tell me about her."

Dutton glanced at the image. "She's been with me for two years. She handles all the claims and billing as well as obtaining explanation of benefits from the insurance companies and posting payments to accounts."

"She would have the ability to doctor those documents before you saw them and dummy up any reports that you might receive?"

His face fell as he obviously realized Colby's line of thinking. "She would. Do you now suspect she's involved with this?"

"I know she is. Moments before this photo was taken, she hit Brooke over the head and stuffed her into the trunk of that car. Where would she take her?"

"I don't know. Honestly, I don't know. If she's involved in this, it's without my knowledge. I had no idea this was going on."

"She couldn't have pulled this off herself. Who would have helped her? Have you ever seen her with a man? A boyfriend? Anyone who seemed suspicious?"

"Ross Benton. The two of them are close. She was the one who recommended him for a job when our IT person had to leave last year. Now that I think about it, I tried to convince the previous guy to stay, but he seemed scared. He was being harassed and wanted to move his family away. He didn't even work out his resignation. Ross started the very next day."

Colby leaned back in his seat. This guy sounded like someone they needed to look into. He messaged Olivia, asking her to focus on Ross Benton's background.

"You said Ross and Sheila are close. What do you know about them? Their personal lives? Their politics?"

"I don't generally ask about such things. They are both quiet and keep to themselves. I got the impression they're involved, but I've never pried. They do their jobs and, as far as I can tell, they are good workers. I've had no complaints about them. Some people think Ross isn't the friendliest person, but other than that, there have been no serious complaints about him."

Colby's phone buzzed and he glanced down at the text from Olivia telling him she had something he needed to see.

He gathered up the files. "Thank you for your help, Mr. Dutton. I'll have someone take you back to your cell."

"How long do I have to remain here?"

"As of right now, you're still being charged with healthcare fraud. Until we can prove Sheila and Ross are behind it, you're still on the hook."

He hurried back upstairs and pushed open the door. Ross Benton's face was big on the screen, along with his rap sheet, which included multiple instances of assault, robbery and aggravated assault.

"Check this out," Olivia stated. "It looks like Ross Benton is an alias. His real name is Ross Frampton. He was arrested two years ago along with Travis Taylor, a known associate with ties to the Freedom from Government Interference, a homegrown organization with ideologies that government is responsible for all the ills of the world. The authorities believe they were involved in planting a bomb at a federal building. It apparently malfunctioned and didn't go off. They managed to escape but were captured on video surveillance and have been wanted for questioning."

Colby didn't like what he was seeing. This guy Ross was bad news. This was their tie-in to the radical extremists. If what Dutton had told him was true, Sheila had brought Ross in to work at Healthmax. They were likely using the fraudulent billing practices to fund their terrorist ideologies and attacks against government targets.

That didn't bode well for Brooke. She was in the hands of dangerous people. "I want to know where Benton would go. Does he own property? What's his last known address? Anything that can help us pinpoint where he might have taken Brooke."

He paced in front of the screen as Olivia sorted

through information that popped up on Benton. "It looks like there's a utility bill in his name for a rural property on the outskirts of Dallas. According to the deed, it used to belong to Benton's grandfather. It was abandoned for years until they reconnected the utilities a year ago."

"That has to be where they're holed up." Colby picked up the phone and arranged for a team to get ready to head to the address Olivia provided.

"I'm coming too," she told him.

He nodded, and she hurried to fetch her gear.

As he gathered his own equipment, he sent up a silent prayer that they would find Brooke before it was too late. He couldn't let another woman he loved be murdered on his watch, especially not this woman. His heart wrenched at the thought of losing her. He needed her back so he could tell her just how much he loved her and that he wanted to build a life with her. He wouldn't allow her to push him away again.

He tried not to focus on all the things he wanted with her. That would only cloud his decision-making abilities. He needed to be at his best on this raid. He had to remain cool and collected. Brooke's life depended on it.

He loaded his gear into his SUV. Olivia followed along and climbed in beside him as he slid behind the wheel. He put it into gear, turned on the sirens and took off. He prayed all the way that they would be able to retrieve Brooke safely.

Ross's fingers dug into Brooke's arm as he led her back into the house. He shoved her to the floor and taped her hands to the leg of the dining room table.

He turned to Sheila, who still had the gun trained on her. "Try to do a better job of watching her this time."

Sheila nodded, but her face reddened with humiliation. Brooke didn't know if it was because she'd allowed Brooke to escape or because she didn't like being spoken to like she was incompetent. It didn't make a difference. Brooke had no sympathy left for Sheila since she'd learned she was the one to murder Tessa.

Ross texted someone on his phone. "I sent Marcus a message. Once he responds and lets us know where to meet up, we'll leave."

They were waiting on instructions from their group's leader, which meant they were now on a time table. She had to figure out how to escape before it was time to go. She closed her eyes and tried to concentrate on her breathing. Her hands were tied to the table, and she wasn't getting past Sheila without a fight for that gun…something she wasn't entirely certain she could win. Especially since she would then have to tackle Ross if she did.

The feeling of a countdown was overwhelming. There was still so much she hadn't done with her life. She wasn't ready to lose it yet.

The idea of how much time she'd wasted without telling Colby how much she loved him pained her. She did love him with all her heart. Why hadn't she told him when she had the chance when he'd poured out his feelings for her? Instead, she'd pushed him away and accused him of not knowing his own feelings.

She no longer cared what his feelings for Tessa were or had been. She was gone. Brooke was here. She should have acted while she still could. Now, she didn't know if she would ever see Colby again. He was certainly looking for her. She had no doubt of that. But would he find her before whatever these two and their extremist groupies had planned for her?

God, please help me.

He was her only hope now. She might not survive this, but she didn't have to go through it alone. Colby's words reminded her that while God might not always bring them out of danger, He was always with them. That gave her comfort. Colby had been right about something else too. Without even realizing it, God had led her to everything she'd ever wanted out of life— a home, a family and someone who loved her unconditionally. God had given her everything she'd ever wanted, but she'd messed it up. She'd rejected everything He'd offered her.

God, please forgive me. I need You.

If she had to die, she didn't have to go through it alone.

A ding sounded and Ross looked at his phone. "It's time. I've got the location where we're to meet with Marcus."

"Good." Sheila glanced at Brooke. "What do they want us to do with her?"

"We're supposed to bring her. Marcus will take care of her."

Brooke pulled hopelessly at her binds. She knew what that meant. At best, she was probably looking forward to a public execution to energize the group and keep them on mission. At worst, months or years spent as a captive used for leverage and whatever their sick minds wanted of her.

Ross used his knife to cut the tape holding her to the table. Her hands were still taped together, but she was free to get up, and he yanked her to her feet. "Let's go."

He pulled her outside to the car. Sheila moved their suitcases from the trunk to the back seat, obviously to make room for her in the trunk. Brooke tried to calculate what her best chance was and decided she was better off trying to escape now. If they got her into that trunk, there was no telling if or when she would get another opportunity to escape.

Sirens sounded in the distance.

Both Ross and Sheila glanced up at the sound. This was her chance. She pulled away from Ross's grip and took off running.

Ross swore. "She's getting away!"

She put everything she had into moving her legs and was nearly around the corner of the house when a shot rang out and pain pierced her side. She gasped for air and stumbled. She hit the ground with her knee and fell onto her back as pain flooded her senses. She was barely aware of Ross grabbing the gun from Sheila.

"I'll take care of her."

Brooke watched him move in her direction, the gun shining in the afternoon sunlight.

This was it. This was the moment she died.

The sirens wailed as Colby took a hard right into the driveway of the property they'd discovered.

He spotted a car in front of the old house and two figures standing outside. "There they are!"

He was glad to have fellow agents Grey and Shorter backing him up as the two figures ran to the car, hopped inside and took off. They didn't get far. Grey and Shorter's SUV blocked the drive, cutting off their escape. Colby swung his vehicle and cornered them from the other side. They were pinned in, but that didn't neutralize the threat. The man—Cody assumed it was Benton—opened the car door and came out shooting. The other door opened, and the woman he recognized as Sheila Wilkinson also started firing at them.

Grey and Shorter fired back, but Colby hesitated. "Brooke could be inside the car," he reminded everyone.

He circled around the back of his SUV and used the vehicle for cover as he tried his best to look inside the car. He couldn't see anyone inside, but that didn't mean she wasn't crouched on the floor or in the trunk.

"We've got them pinned down," Shorter shouted, but just as he did, the couple darted into the woods.

"Follow them," Colby commanded his team.

He held up his gun and hurried toward the car as Grey, Shorter and Olivia followed the couple into the trees.

Colby stopped to check the car before following. Brooke wasn't in the back seat. He popped the trunk. It was empty too. Several shots were fired. Colby spun around, scanning the area. If Sheila and Benton had help from the FGI, he and his agents needed to remain on alert.

Colby quickly checked the house and walked back

outside to join his team to search the woods. Suddenly, a figure darted from the tree line.

Benton spotted Colby. He raised his weapon, but Colby shot first, and Benton went down. The gun flew from his hand. Colby hurried over to make certain it wasn't in reach. He used his foot to kick it away as Benton grabbed his shoulder and groaned in pain.

"I've got Benton."

"We've got Sheila," Grey shouted out to him. "We're heading back to the house."

They emerged moments later with a handcuffed Sheila in tow.

Shorter hurried over to cuff Benton as well while Colby held the gun on him until the deed was done. Once it was, he lowered his weapon and breathed a sigh of relief. They had these two, but it looked like they were alone here.

Where was Brooke?

He walked over to Sheila and demanded answers. "Where's Brooke? What did you do to her?"

Sheila looked away and refused to answer.

Gray approached him with a cell phone in his hand. "I took this off of Benton. Looks like he received a text message with coordinates where they were supposed to meet up with their group."

"Nice." Colby put away his weapon. "Call Greg and have him get a team over there to sweep up the rest of the members before they get tired of waiting for these two."

This was their opportunity to end this group's terrorist activities once and for all.

"Colby, here!" Olivia's voice stopped him cold. "There's someone on the ground next to the house."

He hurried around the house. His heart nearly tumbled to his feet when he realized who it was. Brooke. He fell beside her and saw blood on her side near her back. "She's hurt." He took off his jacket and pressed it against her wound.

"I'll get the first-aid kit." Olivia took off running for the SUV. They'd already called the ambulance for Ross, but it couldn't get here soon enough.

Brooke opened her eyes, her lids fluttering. She stared up at him and smiled ever so slightly. "You came. I knew you would."

He rubbed her hair and planted a kiss on her forehead. "Of course, I came. I'm only sorry I didn't get here sooner." He had no idea how long she'd been lying here. He checked her pulse. It was slowing. Not good.

She reached up and stroked his cheek, but her movements were slow and her voice weak. "It doesn't matter. You made it in time for me to say—"

"Brooke, honey, don't wear yourself out. You need to save your strength."

"No. I need to say this. Colby, I love you."

His heart soared at those words he'd waited so long for her to say. He stroked her face. "I love you too, honey." He kissed her lips and pushed her hair back again. "Now, stay with me."

Where was that ambulance?

He glanced back and saw Olivia on the phone. She nodded at him to indicate the paramedics were en route.

He turned back to Brooke. Her skin was pale and

clammy, and the light in her eyes was starting to fade. Blood had already soaked his jacket and the ground beneath her. She'd lost too much blood. She was slipping away fast. She wouldn't last much longer without help.

Fear raced through him. He couldn't lose another woman he cared about. He would never survive that. And living without Brooke seemed like no kind of life at all. How would he ever go on without her now that he'd finally found the woman he wanted to spend the rest of his life with?

He touched her face, tapping her cheeks lightly to keep her alert, but her eyes were cloudy and she was barely conscious. "You have to fight, Brooke. You're no quitter. I know that about you. I love that about you."

Her head moved in a barely visible back-and-forth motion. "I'm no quitter."

"I don't want you to leave me. Do you hear me? I want you to stay here with me in Dallas. I want to marry you."

She gave him a smile that seemed to say yes, that she wanted that too, but he wasn't sure she'd even heard him. He leaned in, kissed her again and whispered a prayer. "God, please don't let her go."

Sirens alerted him to the ambulance that had finally arrived. He stepped back from Brooke and let them treat her, but his fear of losing her wouldn't let him move too far away. He pulled out his phone and called his brother, telling him everything that had happened over the past few hours.

"What's her prognosis?" Josh asked him.

"I don't know. They're still working on her, but it doesn't look good, Josh."

There was stunned silence a moment before his brother cleared his throat. "She'll be fine, Colby. We'll meet you at the hospital as soon as we can. We'll be praying the whole way there."

He felt better having his family praying. God didn't always answer prayers the way Colby wanted, but he knew that whatever happened, he had God on his side, along with his family.

The paramedics loaded Brooke into the ambulance and Olivia took his arm. "I'll drive you to the hospital."

He let her, falling into the passenger's seat of the SUV. He didn't know if the team Greg had sent to apprehend those waiting for Sheila and Ross had been successful or if the extremist group was still at large. None of that mattered to him as much as Brooke mattered. He would find out later. For now, all his concentration and prayers were focused on Brooke staying alive.

Feeling slowly came back to Brooke as consciousness pulled her awake. Pain was the first thing she realized, then smell. Based on the odor of disinfectant and the pain ripping through her gut, she was in the hospital.

She tried to open her eyes, finding the effort difficult. She forced them and saw that she was right. She was in the hospital. But what was she doing there? Oh yes, she'd been shot. Sheila had shot her as she'd tried to run away.

Anger over the attack brought her around. She tried to sit, but strong hands on her shoulders pushed her back to the bed. She opened her eyes completely. Colby was standing over her.

"Take it easy, Brooke. You'll pull out your stitches."

She relaxed against the pillow. Her mouth was dry and raw, but she was glad to see Colby was with her. In those last moments before she'd lost consciousness, he'd been with her, but she wasn't sure if he'd really been there or if she'd only dreamed it. She reached for his hand and held it.

He tightened his grip. "I'm not going anywhere."

His assurance was like a soothing balm against the pain. He must have noticed her distress, because he reached above her and pressed the call button. "It's about time you had something else for the pain."

Something else? As if she'd already had something? "How long have I been here?"

He pulled his chair up to the bed and sat, never letting go of her hand. "Two days. We nearly lost you, Brooke." He tightened his hand around hers. "I nearly lost you."

The events came flooding back to her. "Sheila… She shot me."

"Yes, she did. The bullet lodged in your stomach. They had to perform surgery to remove it."

"Was she…? Did you…? Did you catch her?"

He smiled and nodded. "We did. They're both in custody, as are eight members of their organization, including Timothy Mason and the leader of the group, Marcus Whelan. We intercepted a text message from Benton to him. Instead of meeting up with Benton and Sheila as they'd expected, they were met by a group of fully armed FBI agents. Once in custody, Benton spilled everything. The fraud money they were using to plan missions against government targets, abduction attempts against you ordered by Marcus Whelan. He even confessed to helping Sheila after she murdered Tessa. They're facing all kinds of charges, including health-care fraud, kidnapping and murder. We have everything we need to send them all away for a long, long time."

That was music to her ears. But there was something else that was bugging her. She stared at him. He looked like he hadn't rested in days. "You told me to fight."

He nodded and looked up at her. "I did. I didn't want to lose you."

She took comfort in those words, but there was still something—or someone—between them. "What about Tessa?"

Confusion clouded his expression. "What about her? We caught the people responsible for her death."

"You're obviously still hung up on her. You even called me by her name."

His eyes widened in surprise. "Did I? I'm sorry. I didn't mean to." He wrapped her fingers in his. "I'll admit I felt some responsibility for what happened to Tessa, and I allowed that to consume me. That's over now. I cared about Tessa, but what I feel for you, Brooke, is so much more. I'm in love with you. Only you."

Her heart soared at his declaration, and she realized she'd allowed her fear of being betrayed again to rule her emotions. She believed him.

His blue eyes pinned hers. "You said you loved me.

Did you mean that, or did you say it just because you thought you were going to die?"

The adorable hesitation on his face was priceless. She pulled him to her. She was ready to put aside her anger and fears and be happy. "I meant it. I love you, Colby. I'm sorry. I should have said so before."

"Well, you said it now. That's all that matters to me." He leaned down and kissed her. "Now, there's only one more matter to address. I believe I asked you to stay here and marry me. You never gave me an answer."

She sucked in a breath. She'd thought for sure she'd dreamed that. "You…you want to marry me?"

"I do, Brooke. I want to marry you. If that means I move with you, wherever you need to be, I'm on board with that. I'll go wherever you go. I never want to leave your side again."

"And if I want to stay here and spend my days watching the sun set over Texas?"

A slow smile crossed his face. "Then I plan to be in the rocking chair beside you every night for the rest of my life."

It sounded perfect to her. "Yes, I will absolutely marry you, Colby Avery."

He kissed her again, and this time, she didn't worry about what would come next. The future was still uncertain, but she knew now that she could handle whatever else came as long as she and Colby were together.

* * * * *

Dear Reader,

As always, I am so blessed to have the opportunity to write stories for you. Thank you for joining me for Colby and Brooke's story and continuing on the journey with the Avery siblings in my Cowboy Lawmen series. I hope you fell in love with this couple and are looking forward to the final installment in the series—big brother Josh's story coming up next.

When my writing partner suggested I make my heroine in *Texas Killer Connection* have a look-alike cousin, I jumped at the idea. My grandmother was a twin, and fun fact, my mother and her cousin looked so much alike they were often mistaken for twins. Although I didn't get to play up the resemblance in this story as much as I would have liked, the idea took me back to the days when, as a young teenager, I devoured old Gothic romance books. My favorite stories were always the ones where the heroine was mistaken for her look-alike sister, cousin, or even a complete stranger. Those stories were so much fun! I was thrilled to be able to include that feature in Colby and Brooke's story.

I love hearing from my readers! You can reach out to me at my website www.virginiavaughanonline.com or through the publisher.

God Bless!
Virginia

LOVE INSPIRED

Stories to uplift and inspire

Fall in love with Love Inspired—
inspirational and uplifting stories of faith
and hope. Find strength and comfort in
the bonds of friendship and community.
Revel in the warmth of possibility and the
promise of new beginnings.

Sign up for the Love Inspired newsletter
at **LoveInspired.com** to be the first
to find out about upcoming titles,
special promotions and exclusive content.

CONNECT WITH US AT:

f Facebook.com/LoveInspiredBooks

🐦 Twitter.com/LoveInspiredBks

LISOCIAL2021

Get 4 FREE REWARDS!

We'll send you 2 FREE Books plus 2 FREE Mystery Gifts.

FREE
Value Over
$20

Both the **Love Inspired®** and **Love Inspired® Suspense** series feature compelling novels filled with inspirational romance, faith, forgiveness, and hope.

YES! Please send me 2 FREE novels from the Love Inspired or Love Inspired Suspense series and my 2 FREE gifts (gifts are worth about $10 retail). After receiving them, if I don't wish to receive any more books, I can return the shipping statement marked "cancel." If I don't cancel, I will receive 6 brand-new Love Inspired Larger-Print books or Love Inspired Suspense Larger-Print books every month and be billed just $5.99 each in the U.S. or $6.24 each in Canada. That is a savings of at least 17% off the cover price. It's quite a bargain! Shipping and handling is just 50¢ per book in the U.S. and $1.25 per book in Canada.* I understand that accepting the 2 free books and gifts places me under no obligation to buy anything. I can always return a shipment and cancel at any time. The free books and gifts are mine to keep no matter what I decide.

Choose one: ☐ **Love Inspired**
Larger-Print
(122/322 IDN GNWC)

☐ **Love Inspired Suspense**
Larger-Print
(107/307 IDN GNWN)

Name (please print)

Address   Apt. #

City   State/Province   Zip/Postal Code

Email: Please check this box ☐ if you would like to receive newsletters and promotional emails from Harlequin Enterprises ULC and its affiliates. You can unsubscribe anytime.

Mail to the **Harlequin Reader Service:**
IN U.S.A.: P.O. Box 1341, Buffalo, NY 14240-8531
IN CANADA: P.O. Box 603, Fort Erie, Ontario L2A 5X3

Want to try 2 free books from another series! Call 1-800-873-8635 or visit www.ReaderService.com.

*Terms and prices subject to change without notice. Prices do not include sales taxes, which will be charged (if applicable) based on your state or country of residence. Canadian residents will be charged applicable taxes. Offer not valid in Quebec. This offer is limited to one order per household. Books received may not be as shown. Not valid for current subscribers to the Love Inspired or Love Inspired Suspense series. All orders subject to approval. Credit or debit balances in a customer's account(s) may be offset by any other outstanding balance owed by or to the customer. Please allow 4 to 6 weeks for delivery. Offer available while quantities last.

Your Privacy—Your information is being collected by Harlequin Enterprises ULC, operating as Harlequin Reader Service. For a complete summary of the information we collect, how we use this information and to whom it is disclosed, please visit our privacy notice located at corporate.harlequin.com/privacy-notice. From time to time we may also exchange your personal information with reputable third parties. If you wish to opt out of this sharing of your personal information, please visit readerservice.com/consumerschoice or call 1-800-873-8635. **Notice to California Residents**—Under California law, you have specific rights to control and access your data. For more information on these rights and how to exercise them, visit corporate.harlequin.com/california-privacy.

LIRLIS22

Jeff broke through the trees and saw the climber. She was lying limp on her back in the water. Long blond hair streamed over her face and floated in the water around her shoulders. He couldn't tell if she was breathing.

"Hang on!" he shouted. "I'm coming to get you."

He yanked off his jacket and tossed it on the rocks but didn't pause long enough to unlace his boots. Jeff dived in, surfaced and gasped a breath as the unexpected cold hit his system. Water soaked his clothes, threatening to drag him down. The roar of the falls was deafening.

In two strokes, he was by her side. He slid his right arm beneath her shoulders, pulled her to him and carefully swam her to shore. She gasped a breath and sudden hope filled his heart. He climbed the slippery rocks and pulled her up alongside him. The belay rope was still attached to her harness and he dragged it onto the shore. Then he sat there on the ground, his legs folded beneath him and the woman in his arms. Her chest rose and fell as her breaths stuttered. His hands gently brushed the side of her neck and he felt her fluttering weak pulse beneath his fingertips. So far, so good. Then, for the first time, he really looked into the eyes of the woman he'd rescued. His heart stopped.

"Quinn?" he asked. "Quinn Dukes? Are you hurt?"

Her eyes darted to the top of the waterfall. He followed her gaze, but there was nothing there.

Fear prickled at the back of his neck. Had Paul finally found his home? Was he coming for Addison?

Quinn closed her eyes for a long moment, and he watched her lips move in what looked like a silent prayer.

A siren rose and fell faintly in the distance.

Quinn's eyes widened. "What's that?" she asked.

"My security alarm," Jeff said. One he'd installed in every cabin window in case Paul ever made good on his threats. "Someone's trying to break into my cabin."

Don't miss
Surviving the Wilderness *by Maggie K. Black*
available wherever Love Inspired Suspense
books and ebooks are sold.

LoveInspired.com

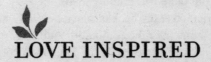